The Other Side of Perfect

Melanie Florence and Richard Scrimger

SCHOLASTIC PRESS / NEW YORK

Copyright © 2022 by Melanie Florence and Richard Scrimger
All rights reserved. Published by Scholastic Press, an imprint of Scholastic Inc.,
Publishers since 1920. SCHOLASTIC, SCHOLASTIC PRESS, and associated logos are trademarks and/or registered trademarks of Scholastic Inc.

First published as *Autumn Bird and the Runaway* in Canada in 2022 by Scholastic Canada Ltd., 604 King Street West, Toronto, Ontario M5V 1E1, Canada.

The publisher does not have any control over and does not assume any responsibility for author or third-party websites or their content.

No part of this publication may be reproduced, stored in a retrieval system, or transmitted in any form or by any means, electronic, mechanical, photocopying, recording, or otherwise, without written permission of the publisher. For information regarding permission, write to Scholastic Inc., Attention: Permissions Department, 557 Broadway, New York, NY 10012.

This book is a work of fiction. Names, characters, places, and incidents are either the product of the authors' imagination or are used fictitiously, and any resemblance to actual persons, living or dead, business establishments, events, or locales is entirely coincidental.

Library of Congress Cataloging-in-Publication Data available

ISBN 978-1-339-002859

10 9 8 7 6 5 4 3 2 1   24 25 26 27 28
Printed in Italy   183
First edition, April 2024
Book design by Maithili Joshi

For Richard and Anne: the two absolute best people
to go on this adventure with
—M. F.

What she said. And to anyone who sees themselves
in this book—*you* are why we wrote it.
—R. S.

CODY

Cody stares at his father's hands.

The hands tell how Dad is feeling. They let Cody know if trouble is coming. That's why he pays attention to them.

So far, things seem fine. The hands are busy, carrying a piece of pizza to his mouth. It's dinnertime. The two of them sit at the small kitchen table under the bare bulb.

Dad slides the last slice of pizza into his mouth, like a sheet of drywall into a truck bed. His jaws chomp up and down. His hands hover in front of his mouth. He licks them and wipes them on his jeans. He grabs the can of beer and lifts it to his mouth. He slurps, chews, swallows.

The pizza box is empty. Cody wants to get up, but the table is jammed against the wall, and he's jammed into the corner seat.

He can't leave until Dad does. And Dad isn't moving. He's drinking and talking.

He's telling another story about a guy named Joe from work.

"Did I ever tell you about Joe and the elevator?" he says, belching.

Cody shakes his head—which is a lie. Dad doesn't have many stories. He's told the elevator one before. It takes a few minutes. Cody tunes out.

The kitchen counter and floor are getting dirty. Cody reminds himself to clean tomorrow, while Dad is out. Dad says cleaning is for girls. Once he caught Cody on his knees washing the kitchen floor and kicked him. Hard. "Don't ever let me catch you doing that again," he said. Now Cody cleans in secret. Does Dad think a mysterious girl sneaks in? Does he even notice?

He's reached the point in the story where Joe steps into the elevator shaft without realizing that the elevator isn't there.

"They're all like that. It's the firewater."

Dad tosses away the empty beer can and goes on with the story. Cody knows what happened. Joe saved himself by grabbing the elevator cable and swinging to safety on the floor below. Which always struck Cody as cool and athletic. But Dad likes to make fun of Joe.

He's laughing now, his hands open on the table. They're like huge shovels, tanned brown, rough skinned. Knuckles like walnuts. Dirt under the nails.

There's a thin wedding ring on the left hand, the nearer one. Cody can't help smiling at the idea of Dad getting married. Wearing the suit, standing at the altar, saying the words, kissing the bride. It's a funny picture. Dad and Mom getting married. Dad and Mom kissing. Dad and Mom doing anything together that didn't involve yelling or throwing things.

Funny. The way choking to death on dessert is funny. The way drowning in a bathtub is funny. The way being crushed by a piñata full of candy is funny. Something that should be good for you, that should be nice, something you look forward to—that thing turning out to be horrible.

Not funny *ha ha*. Funny *oooooh*.

"What are you smiling at?"

Cody snaps to attention. What's happening? What has he missed?

Dad's chair is away from the table. He's frowning like a thunderhead. His hands are on his thighs. Uh-oh.

"I was just, uh, thinking about Joe and the, uh, elevator."

"I finished that story. Now I'm talking about me getting fired and Joe keeping his job. Joe telling me it's too bad I'm behind on rent. A drunken Indian feeling sorry for me. Think that's funny? Do you? Do you think that's funny?"

"I don't. I—"

"You got rocks in your head? Huh? Rocks in there, dumbbell? Dumbhead? Bonehead? Dumb—rock—bone—"

He starts to sputter.

Cody is frightened. But Dad talking gibberish about bones

and rocks and bells is actually funny. Can you be scared and amused at the same time?

Yes. Yes, you can.

But not for long.

Cody stops laughing when his dad hits him.

"Don't laugh at me!"

His face is as red as his hair. Fire red. His hands are not open anymore. They are clenched into fists. The one that hits Cody is the one with the wedding ring. It snaps super fast. Like a snake. Like a mousetrap. It catches him on the cheek—once, twice. His head rings like a bell. A dumbbell. *Ding-dong.* Cody sprawls against the back of his chair. Dad pulls him away from the table and hits him again. And again. Left fist, right fist.

"You laughing now?" he shouts. "Are you? Are you laughing?"

He pushes Cody into the living room. Cody staggers and falls to his hands and knees. He isn't as scared as he was a minute ago. It's too late for scared.

Dad's never been this mad before. Cody knows he should do something. But what? No point in fighting. Dad weighs three times as much as him, and it isn't all fat and beer. Dad's arms are mostly muscle, with those huge fists at the end. What to do?

Apart from not laughing, that is.

Cody's mind is not racing. It's drifting. Like a scene in the movies that's slow motion and out of focus. What to do? *Whaaat toooo dooo?*

There's Dad's fist at the end of his arm. Which makes it about an arm's length away. Here it comes. Now Cody's lying on his back.

There's Dad's shoe on the end of his leg. Which makes it about a leg's length away. Is that a thing?

Cody turns his head. There's the door. Think about that.

Think about going out the door. Think about doing that.

Here comes the shoe. Cody's world goes black.

AUTUMN

Autumn was scared.

It was a heart-pounding, cold-sweating, hands-shaking, bone-deep terror. She literally felt like her heart was going to pound out of her chest. That couldn't really happen, right?

God, she felt like she was about to have a heart attack. Maybe someone would find her, draped across her bed like some old-timey movie star in those black-and-white films her parents loved, dead in the Wonder Woman Underoos she stuffed into the very depths of her top drawer whenever a friend slept over. She could see the obituary now:

> *Thirteen-year-old girl found dead in her home of apparent heart attack, in superhero underwear, because she was going on her first date and her heart couldn't take the utter stress and anxiety of it all.*

Text notifications kept going off. She threw herself across the bed to grab her phone.

> **Are you almost ready?**

Mia. And no. She wasn't. Not unless Connor was okay with her showing up at his place in her underwear. Actually, from what she had heard about him, he probably was.

Oh God.

She had to be there in two hours. It seemed like a huge amount of time, but not in the circles Autumn found herself circulating these days. She was well aware that if she could just throw on a pair of jeans, leave her hair in a messy bun, and wear her glasses instead of the dreaded contact lenses that felt like they were constantly gluing themselves to her eyeballs, she actually *could* be ready in twenty minutes. But the thought of what her friends would say if she showed up without making herself look absolutely perfect, just to hang out at someone's house, catapulted her off the bed and into the shower.

There was a pretty lengthy checklist Autumn followed to get ready every morning, but prepping herself for a party was even more complicated. She shampooed her hair twice and then conditioned with the expensive Aveda conditioner her friends swore made their hair grow two inches a month. She stepped out of the shower, wrapped a blanket-sized bath towel around herself, and leaned across the counter to put her contact lenses in. She still struggled with them. How did anyone *not* blink uncontrollably when they tried to stick something in their eye? But she had begged and pleaded with her parents to let her try them, and there was no way she was going to wear her dorky glasses outside the house unless she got pink eye or something.

On second thought, she'd definitely stay home if she got pink eye. Something like that could lose you your spot at the lunch table quicker than you could say, "Do you watch *Doctor Who?*"

Thinking of being at the get-together tonight as Connor's date made her suddenly wish for a raging case of pink eye. Probably not how you were supposed to feel about going out with the most popular boy in school.

Autumn studied herself in the mirror. Her face was clear. She thought she had nice eyes. And she'd always liked her long, dark hair, like her mother's. But in middle school, that wasn't enough anymore. Autumn blow-dried her hair in sections with a big round brush, then followed that up with a curling iron to get her stick-straight hair to fall in soft beachy waves on her shoulders. When that was perfect, she opened her makeup bag and started on her face. Her parents hated her wearing makeup, so the trick was to keep it as light and natural as possible. But she was going to a party. And on a date! She had to look especially good tonight. A little tinted moisturizer to make her skin glow. And since it was a party, she brushed some highlighter on her cheekbones and touched her eyelids with a little shadow.

Mascara on her lashes, and a quick slick of pink gloss on her lips. There. She nodded at her reflection.

Last, Autumn had to pick out her clothes. That was probably the most stressful part of getting ready. Autumn had never really been into clothes. She'd be perfectly happy slouching her way to school wearing a Spider-Man T-shirt, flannel pajama pants, and her scuffed Chucks, or throwing on an oversized comfy sweater for a party.

But that's not how girls like Autumn were supposed to dress.

Autumn had somehow managed to become one of the popular kids at her school. She wasn't even sure how it happened. But the popular girls did not wear Spider-Man T-shirts. The popular girls wore designer jeans and cute tops from Forever 21. The popular girls turned heads. And you didn't turn heads in pajama pants and Chucks. You didn't go out with guys like Connor unless you put an extraordinary amount of effort into your appearance.

It was absolutely exhausting being popular.

CODY

Cody opened his eyes with a gasp of pain. Ouch!

You knew you were in trouble when it hurt just to open your eyes.

It took him a moment to work out where he was. Oh yeah. The living room floor. No idea how long he'd been lying there. There was a little daylight left, so not too long.

Back to *ouch*. Cody felt like the school soccer team had been using his head as the ball, kicking it all over the field. Come to think of it, *ouch* wasn't strong enough for how bad he felt. More like *AUUUGH!* Or maybe the way those excited foreign sportscasters celebrated: *Goooooooooooooooooal!*

He remembered how he'd gotten there. Dad.

Was the old man still around? Cody listened hard. He heard the tick of the kitchen clock and a rustle from maybe mice. But that was all. No swears or snores. Dad was out somewhere. Cody was on his stomach. He moved his hands into a push-up position and tried to lift. He couldn't do it. He tried again. He had to pee, and he'd rather do it in the toilet than his pants.

One, two, three. Lift. He made it onto his hands and knees.

The soccer team took a corner kick with his head. Another *goooooal*! He crawled to the bathroom.

He pulled himself to his feet with a little help from the sink, but he wasn't ready to pee standing up yet, so he sat down. Good news: He didn't fall over.

Feeling a little better, he leaned over the sink to wash his hands and face. He checked the inside of his mouth with his tongue. One loose tooth at the back. He cupped his hands to take a drink, swishing water around his mouth and spitting pink. Oh well.

His soccer headache was going into extra time. Cody grabbed the big bottle of ibuprofen. There wasn't much else in the medicine cabinet except mold. Dad always took a handful of pain pills at once. Cody tried three.

Straightening up, he caught sight of himself in the mirror. *Sheesh!*

He'd been beat up before, but never like this. No wonder he hurt so much. Both eyes were darkening, on their way to black. His nose was swollen. There was blood smeared across his forehead and cheek.

Cody was so startled by his appearance, he made a decision. He had to get out of there. And he had to do it now, while Dad was out.

One decision led to others. If Cody was running away, he'd

need stuff. He staggered back to the living room. He kept his belongings in a plastic tray under the couch. He slid out the tray and picked a T-shirt, a sweatshirt, a pair of underpants, and a twenty-dollar bill he'd been saving in the small pocket of his other pair of pants. He crammed everything into his backpack and stood up again. Anything else?

In movies, kids running away from home bring along something sentimental to stare at later. A photo, a book, a birthday card. Cody didn't have anything like that. He folded some ibuprofen pills into a square of toilet paper and stuffed it in his pocket. Pain relief—better than a warm memory.

He grabbed his jacket from a hook in the hall, shook it, stepped on the cockroach that fell out, and left the apartment, closing the door quietly behind him.

Cody waited by the elevator in the dim hallway. Chatty Mrs. Ahmad from 316 passed him on her way to the garbage chute. As usual, she had something to say.

"So you're taking the lazy way down tonight, eh?"

He nodded, turning away.

He was using the elevator because he was too hurt to walk down three flights of stairs, but he didn't want to admit it. Never talk about your business. It was a rule. Cody remembered the questions after his mom went away. He and Dad never answered any of them.

The elevator doors opened. Cody stepped on carefully.

"Oh! Oh dear!" She was staring at him.

Dad made fun of Mrs. Ahmad, called her a towelhead. She wore the kind of covering where you could still see her face. As the doors closed and the car started down, Cody was left with the image of her looking concerned and sad and helpless, a bag of garbage dangling from one hand. Ground floor. He stumbled across the lobby and out the door of the apartment tower. He was moving on instinct, like an animal. *Get away from the threat.* Get away from the apartment, from the building, from the neighborhood. Get away from his life here, from the home he knew and feared, from his dad. Cody was not running toward anything. He was running away.

Images and thoughts flickered across his brain like magic shadows on a wall: *Here's the front walk. Don't trip on the loose tile. Here's the street. Lights, noise, people, traffic. Cross at the crosswalk. Look left, look right. Step out onto the road.*

Oops!

Step back onto the sidewalk. Horns. Brakes. Shouts.

"Watch out, jerk!"

Cody pressed the button to make the lights flash. Staggered to the other side of the street, turned left, and kept going. The cemetery on his right looked peaceful in the evening light. Cody wouldn't mind resting there, but it was too close to home.

Keep moving.

His backpack felt heavier than usual. Must be the extra clothes.

At the top of the street, he turned right by instinct. This was the way to school. He crossed the bridge with cars zooming by on his left and ravine shadows staying still on his right. He focused on his steps. Left. Right. Breathe. Left. Right. Breathe. He was drifting. He rested against a lamppost. Deep breaths. In, out, in, out. He pushed on again. Left, right, breathe, keeping his mouth open because he couldn't breathe through his nose.

His head still hurt, but not like before. It was just a regular headache now. The painkillers were working.

He reached the intersection at the end of the bridge. The light changed. He stopped. What now? Keep going to school? Or turn left?

Cody lived in one of the poorest neighborhoods downtown. Tens of thousands of people just like him crammed their whole lives—pots and pans, pets and poverty—into a few crumbling blocks. Some of their windows faced a ravine to the north. On the other side of that ravine was one of the richest neighborhoods in, like, the world.

Cody knew the neighborhood. He had wandered through it, wondering what it would be like to live there. Seemed like every house had a west wing, five chimneys, and a butler.

The intersection marked one end of Cody's neighborhood. He was literally at a crossroads. His school was ahead and to the right. He could go there, but the traffic light was red. The signal with the hand up told him to stop. To his left, across Bloor Street, was the start of the rich neighborhood. That light was green. The signal with the walking figure told him to go.

Without making a conscious decision, he obeyed the traffic signs and headed to his left. Bloor Street was six lanes wide at this point. Cody crossed them all and kept walking, past the subway station, up the hill, and into the rich neighborhood.

The sidewalks seemed so wide here. Cody spotted a bird, a dark silhouette against the gray sky. And another bird, smaller, flapping. And a small, quick, flitty shape near a tree—a bat. He shivered. He hated bats. Speaking of shivering, the air was cooler now. Almost chilly. Cody was glad he was wearing a jacket.

An old lady was walking her dog toward him, her skin and hair very white, her dog's fur very black on the end of the leash. When she saw Cody, she pulled her dog to the other side of the road.

Not too many other people were out. A sports car drove by with music blaring. Cody didn't recognize the music. He didn't belong here. The lady with the dog knew that. He couldn't imagine staying here any more than he could imagine staying in Hollywood or Hobbiton or Hogwarts, but he knew the layout. There were nooks where he could hide once it got dark. There were soft lawns to stretch out.

He stopped mid-yawn. His jaw hurt. Was it bedtime? It seemed like it. Cody didn't know the actual time. He didn't wear a watch or carry a phone.

Phone—ha ha. He remembered lunch last week at school, the whole table of kids comparing their new phones. Cody had walked by without stopping. How would he ever get a phone? Who would pay for it? Dad complained at the cost of pizza.

Some of those kids might live around here. If they did, Cody might end up walking with them to school tomorrow. That would be awkward.

Cody's brain was flickering in and out again. He struggled to focus his thoughts. It was still Thursday, right? So tomorrow was Friday. School gave Cody a place to spend the day. Which was good. But if Dad was looking for him, school was where he'd look. Which was a problem.

Or . . . was it? Would Dad look for him? Would Dad miss him at all? Would he even know he was gone? You know, he might not. He'd forget beating Cody up—he always did. He might forget him entirely for a few days.

Dad. Won't. Miss. Me. Cody was happy at the thought. No,

he wasn't. Well, maybe he was. He didn't know how he felt, except tired and sore. He started to yawn, catching himself before his jaw hurt again. He stumbled around the next turn and started looking for a place to spend the night.

There was a house with a pointy, round turret. Beside it was a house with a sculpture on the front lawn. Between the houses was a thick hedge that smelled like salad. Sort of spicy. Cody inhaled deeply, stumbled, spun around, and fell sideways into the hedge.

Dad won't miss me. I won't miss him.

Cody ran out of energy. The internal mechanism of heart and mind, fear and pain, need and hope, the human engine, ground to a halt. He wriggled out of his backpack and slid down the hedge to sit on the ground with his head slumped forward onto his chest. He closed his eyes.

Footsteps.

Cody startled awake. Someone was walking toward him. The streetlight shone from behind the stranger's head like a halo. Was this an angel? The figure came closer and turned into a girl he knew from last period, social studies. One of the rich cool kids. What was her name again?

Autumn.

AUTUMN

"OHMYGOD!" Autumn shrieked and jumped backward pretty gracefully for someone who had narrowly avoided a dead body.

She had nearly stepped on him before she actually saw him. After cutting through the lot where the rebuild was going on, she turned onto the sidewalk and there he was—some homeless guy, curled up and hidden pretty well by the hedge.

He looked dead.

There was a dead guy lying right in front of her.

There was a dead guy lying right in front of her and she had absolutely no idea what she should do.

Crap.

Fight or flight? She was sweating, and her heart was pounding. She wasn't sure she even *could* run away. But she knew to call 911 in an emergency, and a dead person at your feet definitely qualified. She had to call the police. And her stupid phone was blowing up because she was already late for the party. She tried to unlock it, but her hands were shaking so much she dropped it. Beside the dead guy.

Holy crap.

Her phone was TOUCHING him!

There was no way she was going to reach down to get it. She had seen enough horror movies to know that the dead guy comes back to life the second you let your guard down or get too close. She reached a toe out and tried to pull it back but nudged the guy in the back by mistake.

He moaned.

Crap on a cracker!

She swiped a hand down and grabbed for her phone desperately. He was twitching, but she didn't want to wait around for him to, like, leap up and attack. She turned and ran back toward home even as the guy's face registered in her head. She dashed through the shrubs, stabbing at her phone screen, and then stopped. She knew him.

He went to her school!

Tony. Or Toby. Or something like that.

"Hey." She inched back toward him. "Hey! Wake up!" She reached his corpse-like body and wrinkled her nose. He *smelled* dead. He clearly hadn't showered lately. She nudged him with the toe of her shoe. Nothing. She shoved him hard enough with her foot to jostle him to one side.

"Whattheheckareyoudoing?" he mumbled, rubbing his eyes. Jeez. He had either been in a fight or someone had mugged him. Her phone lit up for the millionth time, then started ringing. Great. Mia always switched to calling if Autumn didn't answer her texts fast enough. And she was always mad about it.

"Autumn! Where the heck are you? You're late. You know I hate waiting." Mia didn't even give her a chance to respond. And the half dead kid was mumbling something she couldn't make out.

"Shh," she told him.

"Autumn Bird, are you shushing me?" Mia shrieked.

"No! Sorry. I . . . stubbed my toe. I was . . . hissing in pain."

"What is that? Are you with someone else?"

"No!" Autumn shot daggers at the kid. If he would just be quiet for one second. "Mia, I have to go. Something came up. Just tell everyone I'll see them tomorrow."

"Autumn!" Mia was about to launch into one of her famous guilt lectures and Autumn had bigger things to worry about. Like the guy grimacing in pain at her feet.

She took another look at Toby or whatever his name was and hung up, knowing she'd pay for it later.

Her phone immediately started going off again, but she stuffed it in her pocket and looked down at the boy, who had sat up and was looking at her distrustfully.

"Look, I don't know what happened to you, but you can't stay here. Someone's going to call the cops."

"I'll leave," he muttered, struggling to his feet and wincing.

"You go to my school," Autumn told him. "What's your name?"

"Cody."

Cody. Right. He was always getting into trouble for being late or not handing in forms or swearing. Basically, a loser. Definitely not the kind of kid her friends would even acknowledge, let alone speak to. She watched him gingerly touch the side of his face. It was purple and swollen. His eyes were both black, and his lip was split. And Autumn had absolutely no idea what to do.

"I think you need a doctor," she said passively. Pretty obvious he did. He looked like he had been hit by a car or something.

"I'm okay."

"With all due respect, you look awful. Did you get in a fight?"

He snorted. "Not exactly."

"Well . . . if you won't go to a doctor . . . you can't sleep out here. Can you get home? Do you need me to call you an Uber?"

He laughed bitterly. "Are you going to pay for that?"

"Look, I'm just trying to help."

"You can help me by leaving me alone." He started walking away, looking down the street as if trying to decide where to go next. Good riddance. If she hurried, Autumn could still get to Connor's. She watched him limping away, looking like a dog someone had kicked. If he had a concussion, he could pass out. Or worse. He could die, and she'd be to blame for letting him go off alone.

Autumn sighed. There was no way she could just let him stagger off. Not when he looked like he wouldn't make it another five steps.

"Hey. Cody. My house is nearby . . . I don't know . . . maybe we have an ice pack? Food? Just come back, okay?"

He turned and studied her. God, he looked awful.

"Why?"

"Why what?"

"Why would you want to help me? You've never said a word to me at school. I've seen you with your friends. You cross the hall to avoid me. Why would you help me now?"

She nodded. He was right. And she was a little ashamed of it, if she was being honest.

"Because my parents taught me to help people who need it."

He frowned, then winced in pain. "I don't need your charity."

Okay. She was actually missing a party for this!

"Listen. You look like you're about to pass out. You maybe have a concussion and you're bleeding. Do you want to come and get cleaned up or not?" She crossed her arms over her chest and stared at him. He stood tall for a second and then slumped as he nodded.

"Yeah. Okay."

"Then let's go."

Autumn led them back the way she'd come. It took longer this time because he was limping. She reached out a steadying hand, ignoring the unwashed smell coming off him.

CODY

Cody staggered down the street. He could hardly hold himself up. Good thing she was there.

She. Autumn.

One of the rich kids. The snooty kids. Her and Mia, Fleur and Aliyah and Toby and Jaden and the rest of that crowd. The kids who sat at the window tables of the cafeteria. Kids who hated him. No, that wasn't right. Kids who couldn't be bothered to hate him. Kids who ignored him, who walked past him in the halls as if he wasn't there.

Well, Autumn was not ignoring him now. She was walking with him. She still didn't like him. He could tell. She had one arm around his shoulders, holding him up, but she was leaning as far away from him as she could—like she was afraid to catch whatever disease he had. Being poor, maybe?

Or maybe he smelled bad.

Too bad, snooty girl. Welcome to my world.

He staggered and almost fell. She gripped him harder. It helped that she was a head taller than him. His breath came in rasps.

"We're almost there," she said. "Just two more houses."

Mind you, in this neighborhood two houses meant like a block. *Imagine having a front yard so big you got tired walking across it,* Cody thought. He concentrated on breathing, on putting one foot in front of the other. Good thing he wasn't carrying anything.

Wait a minute!

He stopped. "My backpack. I had a backpack."

When did he have it last? He turned to look over his shoulder. He had been sitting on it, way back there in the hedge. Crap. He was so tired.

"You mean this?" She held out her free hand. The backpack dangled. She'd been carrying it all along. And supporting him too. She wasn't even out of breath.

Sheesh. Wonder Woman.

He set off again. Left foot. Right foot. Left foot. It was night but pretty light out, thanks to the streetlights and the full moon on his left.

He let Autumn keep on carrying the backpack. He wouldn't thank her, though. What did she say—she was helping those in need. Well, he was in need. No point in thanking someone for doing what they were supposed to.

Cody imagined his dad saying, *You have to help people in need.* He would laugh if he was feeling better. Nothing like that could ever come out of his dad's mouth. *You have to bring me a beer. You have to phone my boss and say I'm not coming in. You have to stay still while I hit you.* Those were the sorts of things his dad said.

"Here we are."

She pulled him off the sidewalk. The path was slightly uphill and felt like crushed gravel. The house loomed ahead of him, dark and shadowy except for a lighted window somewhere way up in the air—the penthouse or bell tower or something. Holy crap, the way some people lived.

Around the side of the house things got clearer. They were on a winding driveway, coming up to a covered porch with a fancy gas lamp hanging from the ceiling. The lamp threw a yellowy light so the scene looked like an old-fashioned painting. Autumn started to lead him up the steps.

"Wait!" Cody's instinct was strong here. "Don't tell anyone about me."

"You're in bad shape. I want to ask my mom if—"

"No." He pulled away from her.

"But my mother can help you, she's—"

"No!" he whispered fiercely. "No parents."

If her parents found out his name, there would be phone calls and excuses. Next thing they'd be driving him home, back to Dad. Anything would be better than that. He leaned forward and grabbed his backpack from her and slung it over his shoulder.

"I'm not talking to any parents."

He took staggering step away from the porch.

"Stop!" she said. He turned, slowly. She had her hands up in front of her face, like she was surrendering. "Okay, there's a place. You can stay in the studio. It's out back behind the house. I won't tell anyone."

"No parents?"

"No parents. My dad works there. You can stay the night."

"Okay."

She led him past the porch and around the corner into the backyard. It was dark. She took out her phone and used the flashlight to guide them. In a voice that sounded angry and somehow amused, she said, "I'm trying to help you, Cody. I don't know why you get to make the rules."

"Because I'm the one running away from home."

They stopped in front of a building. It was too big for a shed. What had she called it—a studio. Was that like a garage? A cottage? Was it where the servants lived? Cody tried to think back to TV shows about rich kids.

The door was locked but Autumn had a key. She led the way inside.

"No lights," he said. "Keep using your phone."

There was a funny smell. Sharp and clean, but not soapy or

like a swimming pool. Kind of a cool smell. Cody stayed still. He didn't want to bump into furniture or statues or dinosaur bones or chariots or whatever they had in there.

Autumn walked into the middle of the room and shone her light into a corner where there was a couch with a blanket on it.

"Is this okay?" she asked. "Or do you have a rule about sleeping on sofas?"

"Ha ha."

Cody had never liked Autumn. But she had *something*. First, caring enough to pick him up off the street, then bringing him here, and then teasing him. Not everyone would do that.

The couch was dark leather—lumpy and dusty and pretty comfy. He relaxed, slumping back and sliding around so he was lying down with his head on one of the arms. This was the best he'd felt since dinner.

"Thanks." The word slid out before he could stop himself. He wasn't going to thank her. But she had gone to some trouble. He felt a lot better. And that was something.

He could hear angry chattering. Raccoons, probably. And a barking dog, somewhere. Cody shivered—he didn't like dogs.

"Hey," she said softly. Her phone light was right in his eyes, making him blink. "Hey, how's your face? Whatever happened to you—it's none of my business. But your face is . . . I mean, is that why you're running away?"

He didn't know how to answer. How could he explain his life to her? Anything he said would make him look like a total loser. Which he didn't want to do. And how could she possibly understand, anyway? No one who lived like she did could understand. Also, he was afraid that if he did start an explanation, he wouldn't know how to stop.

"I'm really sorry," she said.

"Why? You didn't do it."

"I can still be sorry it happened."

There wasn't much to say to that.

"I'm going to bring some ice for your face," she said. "Bathroom is over there. Will you be here in the morning? Do you have a plan?"

Plan? Cody didn't have a plan. He didn't have a spare pair of socks. He was inside and almost comfortable. That was way better than he thought he'd be doing. If not for Autumn, he'd be out there with the raccoons. His *plan* was to see what happened next.

His eyelids drooped, and he started to drift toward sleep, like a hot-air balloon lifting into the sky. She pulled the blanket from the back of the couch and draped it over him.

Nice of her.

She better not tell her parents about him. She better not.

AUTUMN

Autumn rolled over and pulled the blankets with her, creating a burrito effect that usually calmed her down. But it was hard to relax when you were harboring a runaway in your dad's studio. And she couldn't shake the feeling that he really did have a concussion and she was just leaving him out there all alone.

Couldn't you die from a concussion?

Autumn hauled herself up onto one elbow and looked out the window overlooking the backyard. The studio lights were off, of course. They didn't want anyone to know he was there. She squinted, looking for the dull blue shine of a phone screen. She hadn't seen him with a phone, but she figured he must have one. Didn't everyone these days? Nothing.

She threw the blankets off with a deep sigh of frustration and thrust her feet into her slippers. She wasn't going to get any sleep unless she went out and checked to make sure he was at least still breathing. She shuffled into the hallway and tiptoed past her parents' room, holding her breath and straining to hear any indication that they had heard her sneaking out. But aside from one of them snoring—and they both snored so it was pretty hard to tell who it was—she didn't hear a thing.

Boomer was asleep on the love seat in the hall. He woke up enough to lift his head and sniff but quieted down when she stroked his head and murmured, "Not now."

Autumn stepped carefully over the third step from the bottom, congratulating herself for remembering it was the one that creaked. She let herself out the back quietly and drifted as silently as a ghost across the yard to the studio.

She turned the knob and pushed the door open gently. She didn't even have to step into the studio to hear Cody breathing deeply as he slept. Well, at least he wasn't dead. She closed the door quietly and crept back through the yard, up the stairs, and past her sleeping family, to fall into a deep sleep where she did not dream even once about saving random people by bringing them home with her.

She forgot about him by morning.

Not for long. But she woke up and grabbed her phone, scrolling through texts from her friends and photos of the night she had missed. And then she remembered why she had missed it.

Cody.

Crap.

Autumn was up at her usual ungodly time to get her hair and makeup perfect before school. So if she was lucky, no one else would be up yet. She threw a hoodie over her pajamas and opened her bedroom door. Her parents' door was still closed. A good sign. She led Boomer downstairs, put food in his bowl, and let herself out the back door. The grass was a little wet. She had forgotten her slippers and she felt the grass, cool against her feet. She stopped with her hand on the knob and knocked gently.

She heard a grunt and slipped inside. He wasn't on the sofa. She looked around but didn't see him. She *had* heard him, though. She was sure of it.

"Cody?"

His battered face appeared from behind one of her dad's giant canvases.

"I wasn't sure it was you," he said, sitting on the sofa and dropping his bag on the floor. He looked awful. The side of his face had darkened to a reddish purple and both his eyes were black.

"You need a doctor," she said gently.

"I'm fine."

"You're not fine. You look awful."

He studied her for a second, then shrugged.

"My mom's a doctor. Just come in and let her check you out."

"No parents!"

Autumn flinched.

"Sorry. I just can't go home."

"Someone at home did this to you?" Autumn asked.

"Doesn't matter. Look, I'll leave now and hang out at school. Thanks for letting me stay. I'll find somewhere else tonight."

"Where?" Autumn asked.

"I don't know! Why do you care?"

She didn't know. But she did. Care. Because whatever this kid was dealing with at home was worse than anything she had even seen in movies. Judging by his face, it was bad.

"You can't leave yet. My parents will be getting up and might see you. My mom will leave before me, and my dad will be distracted because, well, he always is in the morning. Just wait, and I'll come get you when it's safe. And it's fine. You can stay here tonight."

"Can you bring me something to eat?" he asked sheepishly. Like someone who wasn't used to having anyone be nice to them. Ever. She nodded and looked up at her parents' bedroom window before heading back to the house.

She did her usual morning routine. Shower. Blow-dry with a round brush, then follow up with a curling iron. Makeup. Clothes.

It was exhausting.

Her parents were in the kitchen when she finally wandered down. Her mom was finishing her coffee while her dad stared at nothing and pulled Boomer's ears.

"Good morning." She smiled.

"You were home early last night," her mom said.

"Yeah, I wasn't really into it."

Mom put her cup in the sink, hugged Dad, then Autumn. "I have surgery late today so I won't be home for dinner."

"No problem." Dad came back from wherever he was inside his head. He stood up. "Let me know when you're on your way and I'll heat something up for you."

He gave her a long goodbye kiss. *Ick*. Parents should NOT kiss.

Autumn grabbed a couple of granola bars and shoved her feet into a pair of boots that looked better on than they felt. Now she just had to make sure her dad didn't look out the window. Boomer saved her by clicking his way across the floor toward the back door.

"You should take him for a walk before you start painting," she said.

"You're right. Soon as I get changed." He headed toward the stairs.

"Kay. Have a good day."

The coast was clear. She grabbed her backpack and headed out to the studio before her dad could get anywhere near a window. Cody was still sitting on the sofa like he hadn't moved an inch since she had left him. She tossed a granola bar at him.

"I have to meet Mia at the end of the street. We always walk to school together." She wasn't sure she could explain to Mia or any of their friends what she was doing with Cody, but she didn't know how to get around it. He shrugged, clearly getting her meaning.

"It's fine. Just get me to the street without your parents seeing me, and I'll get to school myself."

Autumn felt herself blushing. He knew she didn't want to be seen with him. But then, maybe he didn't want to be seen with her either.

"Fine. So there's a house being built on the other side of the street. I'll meet you there after school and get you back into the studio. My dad's usually done working by then, but I'll have to make sure."

"Fine."

He followed her out, letting her lead the way to the street before pushing past her and making his own way toward school.

Autumn shook her head. She didn't know why she was helping this kid. He wasn't very nice, and if her parents found out, she was pretty sure they'd be mad. But he was just so damaged. She watched him go, then turned toward the other end of the street, where Mia would be waiting.

CODY

Cody woke up in a forest. Leaves and sky above him. A stream at his feet. A weird, really old knotted tree right beside him. He blinked. Where . . . What . . . ?

Oh yeah.

Not a real forest. He was sleeping at Autumn's place—a garage or studio or whatever. These were paintings of a forest. Three, four, five of them.

That knotty tree painting leaning against the wall was taller than Cody, and twice as wide. He could practically smell the tree—that's how realistic it looked.

Speaking of which, that smell he couldn't identify in the dark the night before—clean, fresh, not soapy—must have been paint.

The studio was one big open room, with a ceiling that went way, way up, and high windows letting in sun but casting no shadows down on the floor. The big painting of the stream didn't look as real as the others. Maybe it wasn't finished. It was hanging on a stretch of wall with a stepladder beside it, and splashes of color around the edge. Different colors. There was a red so dark it looked like purple mud, another red as bright as a sunny day, and a blue that was almost white.

Cody stared for a full minute. *This* was an amazing way to wake up. He started to yawn—and stopped halfway through because his face was killing him. *That* was a terrible way to wake up. He struggled into the bathroom, found the two pain pills left in his pocket, and washed them down with water from his cupped hands. He caught sight of his face in the bathroom mirror. Both eyes were rimmed in purple and there was a dark bruise on his cheek. He looked exactly like he'd been hit by a car.

Wait! Was that a knock on the door? He darted out of the bathroom, grabbed his backpack, and hid behind the huge painting of the tree.

Then his brain started working. What was he doing? The only one who knew he was here was Autumn. She was the only one who'd knock. When she called his name, he edged out from the painting, feeling like an idiot.

He wanted to say things to her. Like, thank you. Like, what an amazing place this is. Like, why are you being so nice to me? But before he could open his mouth, she got going on how awful he looked and how her mom was a doctor and she should examine him, and wondering who did this to him. As if it was any of her business.

He convinced her not to tell her parents and got her to bring him something to eat. Waiting for her on the couch, he felt awkward. He wasn't used to being with people like Autumn, people who lived so differently from him. He didn't know how to respond. Could they be friends? Was that possible? Maybe not. She came back with a granola bar and told him to get to school on his own. She and Mia always walked together, she said.

He nodded, thinking *of course* Mia lived around here and *of course* she walked to school with Autumn. Mia was the Queen of Cool. Tall, rich, and so sure of herself she never even looked like she was trying. Mia hadn't spoken to Cody all year. Had she even noticed him?

Autumn said she'd meet him after school, and that it was okay to stay another night. He followed her slowly. Would he come back? He had nowhere better to go. He had no plans at all. But . . .

But who wants to take help from someone who looks down on you?

It sucked needing stuff. Maybe he could find a shack in the ravine. Or make one. No one would sneer at him there.

Cody started off ahead of Autumn, but he got hungry halfway down the block and ducked behind a low stone wall to eat in private. It hurt his jaw to chew, and he dropped some of the granola bar, which made him mad because the bar tasted really good. Life was unfair. Everything Autumn had was better than his. Her house, her parents, her clothes—everything. Even her granola bars were better. This one was crammed full of nuts and drizzled with honey. It was salty and sweet, crisp and melty at the same time. It tasted amazing! It probably cost a dollar more than the bars he and his dad had. Just a freaking dollar. It was always the little things that showed the difference.

A wasp buzzed around his head. He waved at it. "No granola for you!" he said.

When he got back onto the sidewalk, he could see Autumn and Mia a block or more ahead of him, in and out of the sunshine as they passed from tree to tree. Autumn looked stronger than Mia, and moved with more energy. She waved her hands around and threw her head back to laugh. Mia looked bored. She nodded a couple of times and put her hand up to her mouth to hide a yawn.

They stopped at the traffic lights on Bloor Street. A block behind them, Cody stopped too. He didn't want to catch up.

When he got to school a couple of minutes later, the yard was full of kids. It was close to the bell. He mooched along the perimeter fence, kicking a small stone in short little passes, right foot to left foot, as if it was a soccer ball.

His face hurt. He would need to ask Autumn for some more ibuprofen once the pills he'd taken this morning wore off completely. He ignored the pain, kept dribbling his stone.

As he neared the basketball court, someone made a wild pass and the ball flew toward him. Cody ducked. The ballplayers laughed, not mean, just thoughtless, as if to say, *Look at the loser.* One of them jogged to retrieve the ball. Cody shrugged and went back to dribbling his small stone until he heard Mia talking.

"Are you sure, Autumn? Really sure?"

Mia had a singsong little girl voice. Cody thought it sounded kind of creepy, but a lot of people liked it, because she had a lot of friends. Aliyah and what's-her-name were nodding along with her now. Cody didn't know what's-her-name's name. She was part of the snooty group. She never spoke. But she nodded at everything Mia said.

Mia and Autumn were standing in the shade of that pine tree the school had planted in the middle of the yard at the start of the year. Part of some eco project. Aliyah and what's-her-name stood behind Mia, leaning toward her. Autumn looked grumpy about something. She was waving her hand in the air.

"Yeah," she said.

"Really, really sure?" asked Mia.

"Really, really."

"Well, that's not what they said last night."

"What?"

"At the party. Remember the party you missed? They were talking about you. Right, Aliyah?"

"Uh-huh," said Aliyah.

What's-her-name nodded vigorously.

"I think you're in trouble," said Mia, leaning forward. "I think you have to make a decision. And if you don't make the right one, you'll get hurt."

Cody stopped playing with his stone. Maybe he didn't like Autumn much, but she had helped him. He owed her. If she was in trouble, he was going to help.

Who was she in trouble with—the snoots? They seemed to be bullying her. There was something in the way Mia said, *You'll get hurt.* She sounded mean. Or as mean as a little girl can sound.

Autumn could sound bossy, like when she said he should see a doctor. But she didn't sound mean.

The bell rang. Cody headed for the double doors at the side of the school along with everyone else. Except for the group of girls. They were behind him now. He checked back to see if Autumn was okay. And she wasn't.

Mia was about to hit her!

Classic bully technique. Act when the teacher's attention is somewhere else. Mia's hand was aiming at Autumn's head. The expression on her face, the way she was holding her arm, reminded Cody of his dad.

He jumped. "Hey!" he shouted. "Hey!"

Three strides and he was there, tackling Autumn to get her out of Mia's range. Well, he tried to tackle her. It was like tackling a tree. She didn't budge, and he hurt his shoulder. Mia still had her hand up.

"What are you doing?" Autumn asked.

"I didn't want her to hit you," said Cody.

"What?"

"What?"

"What?"

"What?"

They all said it together. Even what's-her-name said it—the first word Cody had ever heard come out of her mouth.

His stomach twisted in knots of embarrassment. The blood rushed to his face. They were all staring at him.

"Who *are* you?" asked Mia, with a superior smile. "I've seen you around, but I know nothing about you. You are the—"

"The dirtiest," Aliyah chimed in, wrinkling her nose.

"Really," said Mia. "Have you seen your face? You need a wash, badly. And so do your jeans. Better save up the quarters. Right, Aliyah?"

"Right. Quarters. For the public laundry. Ha ha ha ha."

What's-her-name laughed too. Laundry is funny.

The yard was emptying. A teacher stared at them from near the doors.

"Mia is my friend, Cody. She wouldn't hit me," said Autumn.

"I was brushing away a wasp, *Cody*," said Mia, with a wicked emphasis on his name. He blushed harder. He could kick himself. But, still, there was something about Mia's expression that reminded him of Dad.

"Not that it's any business of yours," Mia went on. "I don't think Autumn knows you any better than I do, except—wait! She did know who you were."

From the doorway, the teacher yelled at them to get a move on. Cody was eager to get away from one of the most embarrassing moments in his life. But he could still hear Mia's mean, teasing singsong.

"What's going on, Autumn? Is there something you aren't telling us? Something about you and . . . *Cody?*"

Peals of laughter.

He didn't want to hear any more. He turned to leave, nursing his shoulder.

AUTUMN

Why had she helped him?

Like it wasn't bad enough she had to deal with the aftermath of missing what was apparently the party of the year, even if they were just watching a movie. And all the drama that seemed to have come up without her there to keep Mia from fanning the flames with Connor. Now she had to deal with this kid.

Cody.

Who had suddenly jumped to her defense against a wasp and made it known to everyone around them that they knew each other.

Mia was eyeing her suspiciously. And you really didn't want Mia being suspicious. She was like a Rottweiler. Once she got an idea into her head, she'd never let it go.

"Do you know him, Autumn?" Mia asked, her eyes boring into Autumn as if she could read her mind. Autumn looked away, but she knew how guilty that made her look, so she immediately made eye contact.

"Ummm. That guy? No. Why?" *Oh, good, Autumn. That'll throw her off the scent. Sheesh.*

"Well, he seems to know you. And came to your rescue. You're a real Prince Charming, aren't you?" She sneered at Cody, who was ignoring her and looking back at Autumn. *Stop looking at me!* She tried to send him a subliminal message, but it wasn't working.

"We have a class together. That's it." Autumn glanced over at Cody and gestured with her eyes that he should leave. He stared back blankly. *Jeez, what is wrong with him?* Autumn put an arm around Mia and steered her so she was looking the other way, toward where Connor and his friends were standing. "Tell me again what Connor said." She really didn't want to hear it again, but it was a surefire way to get Mia to forget about Cody.

It worked.

"OHMYGOD! So Connor was talking to JP, right? And he told JP that he was ready to make you and him Insta-official!"

"But . . . we've barely spent any time together. Why would he want to be my boyfriend?" Autumn asked. She had zero experience with boys, but she figured, at the very least, she should know something about a boy before she became his girlfriend.

"Girl, please." Mia tossed her hair and laughed. "Connor could have any girl at school, but he wants you. Since you stopped hanging out with the geek squad last year and made an effort, you're hot. And someone like Connor needs a hot girlfriend."

"He's never even taken me out to dinner or anything!" Autumn frowned.

Mia and Aliyah laughed.

"No one goes out to dinner, Autumn. You just hang out together. Go to parties as a couple . . ." Mia looked at Aliyah and smirked. "And you make out."

Autumn felt the blood run out of her face and pool somewhere around her heart, which was beating a million times faster than normal all of a sudden. She hadn't even kissed anyone yet, and if she was being honest, she wasn't sure she wanted to.

"Oh, don't be such a baby, Autumn. I've done way more than make out." Mia smirked.

What's way more than making out? Autumn wondered.

"Well . . . I don't know if I'm ready for that. To be . . . Insta-official. Or whatever."

"Don't act all innocent, Autumn. I told you, Connor said he heard you went pretty far at summer camp."

"And I told you that's not true!" Autumn hadn't even hung out with the boys at camp, so she had no idea who had told him that or if he was just making it up.

"Yeah, well . . . you're one of the most popular girls in school now. And if you want to stay that way, you need a hot boyfriend," Mia told her. "And the way to keep him is to stop being such a little kid. It's no big deal. All the girls do it. And if you won't, then you're not going to be one of us."

Mia and Aliyah walked off without waiting to see if Autumn

was following. She wasn't even clear what the two girls had actually done. Kissing? With tongues? More than that? Whatever Mia was talking about, Autumn was pretty sure she wasn't open to doing it. She liked Connor. She liked the attention she got when he hung around her. But if she was being honest, she didn't think she liked him like *that*.

She felt eyes on her as she stood watching the other girls walk into the school. She turned and saw Cody still standing nearby, studying her like a lab specimen.

"What?" she asked, more aggressively than she had intended.

He tilted his head, which made him look more swollen and bruised somehow.

"Nothing."

He picked up his pace, moving out of earshot.

"You coming, babe?" a voice said behind her. Connor draped an arm over her shoulder and started leading her toward the stairs.

I don't like being called babe, she thought to herself as she plodded along beside him mutely.

And I really don't like where your hand is resting, she thought.

Or the fact that you lied about me to your friends.

But Autumn pasted a smile on her face and let Connor lead her into the school, wishing with all her might that she could find her voice and just say what she thought.

CODY

Cody was used to being ignored. He'd been going to Castle Frank Middle School for a year and a half and had never been stopped in the hall. Which was fine. He didn't look for attention. The kind of attention he got from his dad was no fun. So when people ignored him, Cody was relieved.

That didn't happen this morning. He got lots of second looks. One of the basketball stars—he was so tall he had to duck going into classrooms—bent way down to peer at Cody.

"You okay there?" he asked in a low voice. Well, a quiet one. Actually, his voice was reedy and high-pitched. Cody nodded and pushed past.

He was squatting in front of his locker when the vice principal came over. Cody turned his head to see brown leather shoes with designs at the toe, white athletic socks, and chinos. Farther up there was a brown belt, light blue shirt, dark blue tie, glasses with thick black frames, floppy black hair. It was Mr. Choi.

"Are you Cody Stouffer? Eight B? Ms. Koon's homeroom?"

He nodded.

"Close your locker and come with me, please."

Cody was worried. Mr. Choi was not going to give him an award. He was in some kind of trouble. And the obvious kind had to do with Dad. Did the old man call the school? Was he there? Now?

Cody's muscles tightened. His senses sharpened up. He followed Mr. Choi around a couple of corners, expecting to hear a familiar angry voice at any moment.

He would not let Dad get hold of him. Cody planned his escape. He could outrun Dad, he knew. Probably Mr. Choi too. Okay. Ready . . . set . . .

False alarm. There was no one in the main office except the secretary. Mr. Choi led Cody to his private office and closed his door.

"Don't worry, Cody, you're not in trouble."

He did not relax. He had no reason to believe Mr. Choi.

They stood quietly while the anthem played. They sat down as the principal read the announcements. Teams, clubs, dances, meetings. None of this stuff applied to Cody. He didn't belong to anything.

After the announcements, Mr. Choi leaned forward over his desk, opening his hands like one of those ministers on the praying TV channels.

He asked Cody how he was feeling.

"Fine."

"Fine? That's good. No aches anywhere? No stomachache, for instance? Or, uh, headache?"

"No."

"Great." Mr. Choi smiled. "So, uh, Cody, what happened to your eyes?"

He should have known.

"I fell."

"Fell?"

"Yeah. Down the stairs. At my dad's—my place. It was last night. I hit my face on the bottom step."

Mr. Choi was writing. There was a form with spaces left blank, and he was filling out the form with a red ballpoint pen as Cody spoke.

"Ms. Koon noticed your face on the playground this morning and came to me. She says you had another black eye a few months ago. Is that true?"

"Uhhhh, yeah. That's right. Yeah, I did have one. She asked about it."

Mr. Choi's office window overlooked the expressway, where traffic ran through the Don Valley like a second river. At that time of the morning, the northbound lanes moved more like toothpaste than water, and the southbound cars looked stuck, on the way to who knows where—to the lake, to the sun, to the border, to another town. To freedom.

"How *did* you get that other black eye?"

"Like I told Ms. Koon, a guy came out of a bar, ran into me, and started a fight. He was bigger than me."

Cody shrugged. It was the truth. Maybe not the whole truth, but that was how he got the black eye. What he skipped over was that the guy coming out of the bar was his dad.

"So last night you were running downstairs at home and you fell. Is there carpeting on the stairs at your house?"

"Huh?" Where did Choi think he lived? Mud, scraps of paper, cigarette butts, puddles of mostly dog pee. That's what was on the stairs of his building. That's what he walked on.

"I'm in an apartment building on Parliament Street. I usually take the fire stairs. No carpets. I tripped, that's all."

"So your black eye was an accident."

"Oh, sure."

Mr. Choi put down his pen. "I don't want to embarrass you, but I care about your health. Things can get tricky at home. I know that's true for you, with what happened to your mom and, uh, and all. You can tell me if things are, uh, strained. The school will help. Are you okay, Cody?"

He looked down at his paper. Didn't say anything. The moment stretched.

Cody had two reasons for keeping quiet. First was the basic rule: *Don't tell anyone your business.* Dad taught him that when a neighbor asked where Mom was. Before Cody could open his mouth, Dad had dragged him down the hall. *No one needs to know about us,* he said. *Remember that. Stouffers keep their business to themselves.* This was years ago, the first time Mom went away.

Reason number two was what would happen. Dad was clear on this. *You complain about me, Children's Aid will put you in one of their prisons. They say they're keeping you safe, but it's prison.* He said this last year, after he gave Cody an arm bruise that wouldn't go away. *They drive checkered vans,* Dad said. *You talk about me, start looking out for checkered vans.*

Cody found a smile and tried it on. "I'm fine."

Mr. Choi signed the form and sent him back to class.

The outer office looked as empty as before, but it wasn't. A shapeless bundle of clothes on the bench talked to him.

"Psst, Cody."

He jumped. "Oh, it's you!"

Invisible Isabel. She was in Cody's year, and they spent time together, but he didn't know much about her. Wherever she was, she found a way to disappear into the background, so you'd be surprised to see her. She was famous for it. Once her soccer team had too many players on the field all game long because the referee never noticed Isabel running up and down. Of course, no one passed to her, so it didn't affect the score. Cody tried to avoid attention, but he was an amateur. Isabel was Olympic caliber.

"Ms. Koon called while you were in Mr. Choi's office." Because no one ever realized she was there, Isabel heard everything. "They're worried about you. What happened to your face?"

"I fell."

Isabel spoke in a low voice, but Cody's was loud enough for the secretary to hear. She looked up from her computer.

"Here's a note to get back to class, Cody." And then, "Why, Isabel, I didn't see you. Have you been here long?"

Back in homeroom, Ms. Koon came over to Cody's desk and asked how he was feeling. He said fine. She walked away. Her shoes were the exact same color as the math textbook. Did she plan that?

Math, language arts, biology. Most of the time Cody forgot about his face. Every now and then he did something—scratched his forehead, wiped his cheek—and *that* hurt. Then he remembered.

The lunch bell rang. Cody headed for the cafeteria. He didn't have much to eat. The cafeteria was a place to go.

He walked past the cool table. No one noticed him. He got

some water and found an empty table near the recycling area. The granola bar in his backpack was left over from yesterday. It wasn't the super-tasty kind that Autumn's family got. But it was better than nothing. He was halfway through when he realized he was not alone at the table.

"Psst, Cody."

It was really hard to tell what Isabel looked like. Medium height, medium size, medium skin tone. Dull hair tied into a bun, dull expression.

"Hey, Isabel."

Without seeking each other out, they ended up in a lot of the same places, as if they recognized what they had in common—which was mostly what they were not. Not popular. Not athletic. Not smart. They were both watchers, outsiders.

There was something noticeable about Isabel now. Her dark eyes flashed with interest.

"Want to know what I just heard?" she murmured.

"Whatever." Cody didn't know very many people at school. And he didn't care about any of them. He took a small bite of the granola bar, stretching it out.

"It's about Autumn."

Cody snapped his head around. "What? What did you hear? Tell me."

"Well, well, well. Someone just got interested." Was Isabel smiling? For the life of him, Cody couldn't tell. "I was in the bathroom," she went on, "and you'll never guess what they're all saying about her."

AUTUMN

Everyone was whispering in the halls. Which wasn't really unusual for middle school. But this time they seemed to be whispering about her. Which most definitely was strange since she went out of her way not to do anything whisper worthy.

She distinctly heard her name, then Connor's, then the word *skank*.

Great.

She twirled her combination lock, missing the last number twice before she finally got it open. Autumn could feel people's eyes on her as she shoved her backpack into her locker and pulled out her gym bag. She could feel them on her as she trudged down the hall toward the gym, but she kept her head down. She had the weirdest feeling that if she met someone's eyes, Cody might jump out from behind something and try to come to her defense again.

The second she slipped into the girls' changing room, everyone stopped talking. You could have heard a pin drop. Literally. Every single conversation stopped, and twenty pairs of eyes were suddenly hyperfocused on Autumn.

She grabbed Mia and pulled her around the corner to the showers, turning one on to drown them out.

"Why is everyone talking about me?" she demanded.

Mia twirled a piece of hair around her finger and looked past Autumn.

"Mia!"

"Okay!" She stopped twirling her hair and let it drop. "So when I called you last night, you were on speaker, right?"

Autumn nodded.

"Well, when I was asking when you were coming, Aliyah said she heard a guy in the background."

"What guy?" Autumn asked, knowing exactly which guy had been in the background of that call.

"I don't know. Some guy. And she told Connor."

"She told Connor that some guy was in the background of my call?"

"Right. She thinks you were with another guy instead of with Connor. And with the whole thing about you fooling around with a guy at camp . . ."

"I did NOT fool around with anyone at camp!" Autumn stamped her foot. "How did that rumor even get started?"

"I don't know who started it, but Aliyah told me you had a boyfriend at camp." Mia shrugged.

"OHMYGOD! I didn't have a boyfriend at camp. I did

NOT fool around with anyone. And I definitely wasn't on a date last night. There was an emergency at home and I couldn't go out. That's it."

It was the truth. Mostly. She wasn't about to tell Mia or anyone else about Cody being passed out behind the hedge. Or that she had brought him home and hidden him in her dad's studio. And she sure wasn't about to share that she was going to meet him after school and hide him again tonight.

"I'm not the one who said it," Mia told her, tossing her hair and turning off the shower. Clearly she was done talking.

"Well, maybe you could tell Aliyah that I was home. Alone. And not on a date."

Autumn walked back through the mostly empty changing room and traded her trendy clothes for some running shorts and one of her mom's old concert T-shirts. This one had Green Day on it, and she was suddenly grateful she hadn't worn the Sex Pistols T-shirt. She laced up her running shoes and headed outside.

She stopped at the edge of the track and stretched, feeling her muscles loosen as she shook her legs out. Autumn took a deep breath and started running. Her feet pounded on the track—thud, thud, thudding as she took the first turn and sped up. She passed her classmates, who were mostly shuffling around the track in groups, talking and laughing together. She tuned them out, staring straight ahead and running faster, hearing only her own breathing and the sound of her feet hitting the track, leaving behind the girls who were talking about her, and holding her head up high as she finished her first lap and started her second. She saw a kid sitting alone on the bleachers as she streaked past and recognized that it was Cody before she left him behind too.

CODY

After science, Cody had wanted a moment to think, so he went outside for a second. Just a second. He headed to the bleachers and sat down to think about where he'd spend the night.

Could he trust Autumn to look after him? To keep his secret and not tell her parents? Would he be better off on his own, on the road to another neighborhood? Without her?

A gym class was streaming out of the school onto the track. Oh no. He'd been thinking so hard he'd missed the bell. Now it was next period. Cody should be in French right now. Worrying about irregular *-ir* verbs. *Vouloir, pouvoir, devoir.* As if they mattered.

Hey, was that Autumn? Cody half waved as she flashed by. She could really run fast. She ignored him. 'Course she did.

Cody got up from the bleachers and headed inside. Of course Autumn would ignore him, after what had happened that morning. She was probably sick of looking at him. She'd rather hang out with Mia and Aliyah. There was Mia now—she was in this gym class. She loped awkwardly past him on her long legs. She didn't move with power, like Autumn. Autumn ran like a cheetah. Mia was wobbly, like a baby giraffe.

Cody's inner voice told him to get to class.

What's the matter, got rocks in your head?

That was one of his dad's expressions. Cody tried one of his own.

You can do it. You can.

Which made him smile. The French verb *pouvoir* meant "can." *Je peux.* "I can."

In the doorway, he almost bumped into Connor Herlihy, dressed in gym clothes and cradling one hand under his armpit like it hurt. *Well, well.* Was Isabel's rumor true? Cody stopped a second.

"What are *you* staring at?" Connor asked. Emphasis on the *you*. Meaning, you don't matter. You shouldn't be staring at anything.

Connor Herlihy had pretty much everything going for him. He was athletic and smart and popular. His hair was perfect. His skin was clear. His stomach was ridged with muscles.

Cody's stare had nothing to do with any of this.

Rumor said Autumn's new boyfriend was driving Connor crazy. Invisible Isabel had told him about it. She heard Connor was so mad Autumn liked someone else he had punched a wall. And, from the way he was holding his hand now, the rumor was right.

"You want to say something? Do you? What do you want?"

Connor had a rich, resonant man's voice. Cody envied that too. *Vouloir.* "To want." *Vous voulez.* "You want."

Cody shook his head.

Connor made a spitting sound. "You're such a . . . such a . . ." He couldn't decide what to call Cody, so he shook his head and loped off toward the track.

Nothing, Cody's inner voice told him as he hurried down the hall. *You're a nothing.*

French class had started when he got there. He slipped into his seat at the back of the class. M. Terret, the teacher, usually ignored Cody. Today he stared at him with his bulging eyes. He always looked like a frog. Today, a surprised frog.

"Sorry," said Cody. "I mean, uh, *pardon.*"

Terret said something Cody didn't understand. It was a question. Cody shrugged and said sorry again. Terret repeated the question slowly. This time Cody heard the word *combat.* Terret, who was a pretty good guy, made a gesture like he was throwing a punch. That's right. *Combat* meant "fight." The word was in a dialogue from a couple of weeks ago.

Cody nodded. *"Oui,"* he said, throwing an air punch and hitting himself in the face. For a second, he was pleased with himself for understanding French. Terret grimaced and went back to the blackboard. Then Cody remembered telling Mr. Choi about falling down stairs. Oh well. He didn't know the French for *falling down stairs.*

The girl in front of Cody—what was her name again... Anne Marie or something like that?—frowned over her shoulder. Why was he taking up class time? Cody said *pardon* to her too. She sniffed and turned back around.

After class, Terret came over to Cody's desk. Now he looked like a sad frog.

"*La prochaine fois,*" he said, pointing at Cody's face. Cody knew that meant "next time." He nodded. What was Terret getting at?

"*La prochaine fois, tu dois t'enfuir.*"

Cody didn't know what *enfuir* meant. He frowned. The teacher moved two of his fingers along the desk to look like someone running. Aha. Now Cody got it.

"Run away," he said. "Next time, I must run away."

"*C'est ca.*"

Cody walked to Autumn's place alone, checking up and down the street to see if there was anyone else from school. He was walking west. The afternoon sun was in his eyes. He squinted, turning away to check the front doors and house numbers. It was around here somewhere. Right?

You should have written down the address. What's the matter? You got rocks in your head?

Thanks, Dad.

Cody recognized the hedge where he'd collapsed and Autumn had found him. He was on the right street, and her place was close.

Wow. There was a castle! He hadn't realized how big it was last night. It should have a moat. Who lived in a place like that—Batman?

He kept walking. Was it only last night that he'd run away? He felt like he'd lived a year and a half since then. He wondered if Dad had noticed he wasn't there.

There was a place with a billboard in front. ANOTHER PROJECT BY . . . Autumn said she'd meet him at the construction site across from her place. Was that hers over there? The yellow brick looked right. And there was a building in the backyard. He could see it from the street. Yup, that was Autumn's.

The construction site was empty. Cody wiggled through a gap in the billboard. Autumn was not there. He sat on top of a pile of lumber on the front porch, wishing he had something to eat.

Did Autumn have a practice after school? Sports or music or something that rich kids did? Polo? Sailing? She said she'd meet him here. Had she forgotten?

There was a buzz near his ear. He waved away the fly. No, wait, it was a wasp. Which reminded him of this morning.

He blushed at the memory. What a dumb thing to do, rushing to rescue Autumn when Mia was only waving away the bug.

Or maybe she was with the new boyfriend, whoever he was.

Cody asked himself if he should be doing this at all. Should he be bothering Autumn, sleeping in her dad's studio?

The size of his problem hit him like a punch to the chest. Running away for a day was nothing. Running away for good was a big deal. Could he do it on his own? Getting money during the day so he could eat, sleeping in ravines and parks at night. Could he do it? Could he actually do it?

It was too much to take in. He let his mind go, like he did when his dad hit him. He was not present, neither here nor now. Time passed while he thought of crazy things.

Connor not knowing what to call him. *You're such a . . .*

M. Terret's advice: *You must run away . . .*

Waking up thinking he was in the forest because of that amazing painting, all green and gold and purple . . .

Wild things.

A bird called loudly, bringing Cody out of his trance. He caught a flash of black, white, and blue. A jay? He didn't know any other blue-colored birds. The call sounded like a squeaky door.

He couldn't plan long-term. So how about right now? He got up to wiggle back through the billboard to see if Autumn was coming down the street. Nope.

She did say she'd meet him here, right? What if she forgot? What if she was in the building behind her house, waiting for him? Cody decided to take a quick look. If she wasn't there, he'd come back here and wait.

There was someone in the studio. Standing on tiptoe to peer through the small window on the side of the studio away from the house, Cody could make out a dark shape moving around. Not Autumn. This figure was much bigger and broader. And he moved slower, more deliberately, than Autumn did.

It was a guy. An old guy. He moved toward the wall, did something with his hand, then moved slowly back. He was holding something. Was it a knife? But he wasn't stabbing. It was like the wall was a slice of bread and he was buttering it. What was he doing?

The backs of Cody's legs hurt from standing on tiptoe, but he was too interested to walk away. There was something about this guy and what he was doing. The wall he was buttering was the one with that cool picture of the forest on it. Wait! The guy was Autumn's dad. And he was painting!

Cody's breath caught in his throat. He looked around for

something to stand on. He found a basket, carried it over, and turned it upside down.

He watched how Autumn's dad painted. What he looked at, what he did, how he did it. There was nothing else that interested Cody right now. He forgot about meeting Autumn. He forgot about school, his headache, his father. He had to watch. He had to.

The hand on his shoulder caught him by surprise.

AUTUMN

Autumn had only seen people scream in utter panic in movies. But Cody acted like someone was about to murder him when she gently touched his shoulder to get his attention before her dad snapped out of his artistic trance and noticed him peering through the studio window like some kind of stalker. If people really peed their pants in fright, she was pretty sure Cody now needed a change of clothes.

"SHHHH!" she scream-whispered, ducking to avoid his flailing arms. Jeez, he was like an octopus. "Do you want my dad to hear you?"

"Autumn?" From inside the studio. Too late. Autumn grabbed Cody by the shirt and pulled him down to the ground underneath the window and out of sight. Her dad was opening the window and staring through the screen with his eyes shaded by his hand. "Hey. What are you doing out there?"

"Hi, Dad." She nudged Cody, who was struggling to sit up. "I didn't want to interrupt you while you were on a roll. How's the new piece coming along?"

"Oh!" He looked super happy to be asked, which she knew

he would be. It distracted him long enough for her to reach down and push Cody's hand away from her leg, which he was tapping in an effort to get her attention. "It's going really well, actually. Why don't you come in and I'll show you? You can clean my brushes for me if you want. Remember when you used to do that?" He chuckled and stroked his beard thoughtfully.

"I'm not cleaning your brushes for you, Dad." Autumn laughed. "And I'll check everything out later. Promise. But I have a ton of homework that I need to start or I'll never get it finished before dinner. Mom's late tonight, right?"

"Yup. We decided to order in."

"Pizza?" Autumn asked hopefully.

"Well . . . she said something about sushi this morning." He shuddered. The idea of raw fish had always freaked him out. Autumn loved sushi, but she laughed at the look of horror on his face.

"I'll tell her I've been craving pizza."

"Thanks, love. Go do your homework so we can watch a movie when I come in."

"Okay."

Autumn waited until her dad had closed the window and turned back to his canvas. She watched him for another second to make sure he was focused. Only when she saw him ducking back and forth in front of the painting and stabbing at it with a brush did she look down at Cody, who was still lying under the window.

"You can get up now. Sorry for kicking you. I didn't want him to see you."

"Yeah, that was pretty obvious," he muttered, getting to his feet and following her to the porch.

"I thought I told you to wait for me across the street." She pulled her hair back and secured it in a ponytail with an elastic.

"I did! I thought maybe you forgot and came home. I saw someone in the window and just . . ." He trailed off.

"And decided to watch him?" Autumn stared at him incredulously. For someone who looked like they snuck around a lot, he was pretty clueless. Without waiting for an answer, she pulled the door open and led the way inside. He didn't follow.

"I never saw anyone painting before," he said. Autumn turned and studied him, eyebrows raised.

"You've never seen anyone paint?"

"No. I mean, I have. I've never seen a real artist. Forget it." He scuffed the toe of his ratty sneaker against the doormat.

Autumn sighed. This kid was so weird!

"Are you coming in or what?" What was he waiting for? An engraved invitation? Sheesh.

"Should I take my shoes off?" he asked, stepping gingerly through the door.

"Oh yeah. And definitely leave them where my parents can find them." Autumn tried and failed not to roll her eyes. He already had one shoe off, and she wrinkled her nose at the sight of his big toe poking through a hole in his grubby sock. Come to think of it, everything he had on was pretty filthy. "You'll have to hang out in my room until my dad is done outside," she told him. "You can take a shower if you want." Crap. That sounded rude. But he had a distinct BO thing going on. And he looked like he hadn't seen a bar of soap in a few days. At least. She glanced at Cody, who was staring at the floor, holding his dirty knockoff Converse shoes in his hand. His cheeks were flaming red, and Autumn felt absolutely terrible all of a sudden.

"Are you hungry?" she asked gently. Because if he hadn't showered in a while, he probably hadn't eaten either. "'Cause I'm hungry. Come on. Kitchen's over here."

Autumn led the way to the kitchen before noticing that Cody had stopped dead at the living room.

"Holy crap," he breathed.

CODY

"Holy crap."

It wasn't that Autumn's living room was cooler than his. Most living rooms were cooler than his. Any room where the furniture had all its legs and the windows weren't cracked and the ceiling didn't have a big water stain—any room without beer bottles on the floor, where you could inhale without wincing—was better than his living room. But this was, like, the coolest room Cody had ever been in. It was bigger than the showroom of that warehouse down Parliament Street. And it had almost as much furniture in it. Couches, armchairs, lamps, tables. Bookcases full of books. The rug on the floor had a fringe on both ends and a pattern that made his eyes cross. The walls went up past where the ceiling should be, all the way to the next floor. And they were full of pictures.

One or two of the pictures looked like that forest scene in the studio. There was a giant gray one with an orange triangle and squiggly lines that made Cody feel sad even though he didn't know what it was a picture of. There was one of a parrot and a can of lunch meat that was just weird. On a side table was a piece of wood carved at one end so that it looked like it was turning into an animal, and a bowl of leaves that smelled nice.

The room was enormous, but restful and warm at the same time. It was a room for movie stars and princesses. Cody was amazed—*amazed*—that Autumn lived here.

"What?" she asked.

"You can just wander in here any time."

"What do you mean?" she answered from the kitchen.

He walked carefully over to a painting of a stream. The water frothing over the rocks in the picture was all sorts of colors. He could see green and yellow and even black. But when he stepped back, it looked like regular river water. How did that work?

The name at the bottom right was T. Bird. How did he combine colors that weren't blue to make it look like water?

"Hey, food's ready."

Cody's stomach wouldn't let him keep looking at the painting. He hadn't eaten a full meal since yesterday. He hurried to the kitchen. Autumn had made toast covered with lumpy green paste. Normally Cody wouldn't eat this because it looked weird. But he was too hungry now. He inhaled three pieces.

"Hey, you really like avocado toast, eh?" She was finishing her first piece.

"That what this is?"

She gave him an odd look and stood up. "I'm worried about

Dad. He might come inside early. Let's get you hidden."

She led him to a narrow set of stairs at the back of the kitchen. Upstairs was a big hall with rooms leading off it. The carpeting was soft and deep green and wall to wall. Across the hall was a set of stairs going up to a third floor and down to the first.

"Wait—your place has *two* staircases?"

She turned with a smile. "Yeah."

Funny thing about her smile. It wasn't superior and snooty. It could be, but it wasn't. She could see he was overwhelmed, and she was sharing that feeling.

"Until we moved here, I'd never been in a place with two staircases," she said. "I guess you haven't either."

"Uh, nope."

All the homes Cody had ever visited were in apartment buildings, except that time he and Mom went all the way to the end of the subway line to see a lawyer who worked out of her home, and that was a bungalow. Cody had never been in a house with *one* staircase before, let alone two.

They walked past a bright, sunny room with a desk and computer and a million books in it. A few steps down the hall was a deep blue door. Autumn pushed it open.

"Sorry for the mess. Stay here until I come and get you. My bathroom's through that other door. There's a shower. I'd use it right now." She blushed. "I mean, if you want to. Dad'll be in soon. You have a change of clothes in your backpack, right?" She was looking at the floor now, talking quickly.

Why was she embarrassed? There was no mess in the room at all, unless you counted a pile of books on a little table. Because he'd be showering? No, she was embarrassed for him! She saw his bare toe sticking out. Crap! He slid his foot on the carpet to pull his toe back into the sock. Double crap!

"What's that?" He pointed to a poster over her bed. Blue and white lines on a dark background. It was a plan, like for a building, with arrows and writing—only it wasn't a normal building. It was a kind of closet, with windows. The sign above the door said POLICE PUBLIC CALL BOX. What did that even mean?

She gave a little laugh and said something that sounded like TARDIS.

Which couldn't be right. It wasn't a word. Maybe it meant something in French or Spanish.

Cody was overwhelmed. All this—Autumn's house, her stairs, her bedroom—was too much. He felt like a time traveler from the Middle Ages. He was so over his head that he felt a bit reckless. What else could happen? Could he take control of *anything*?

"Okay, shower time," he said. He pulled off his shirt and reached for the zipper on his pants.

"Whoa there, speedy! Do that in the bathroom—and give

me a chance to get out!" Autumn left her room in a hurry, closing the door firmly behind her.

The shower was actually fun. Cody had no trouble with the sliding glass door or the twisty pull-on faucet or the pump bottle of body wash. He rinsed, shut off the water and found a towel, and didn't make a mess on the tiled floor. Operation: Cody Clean was a huge success.

In the silence after the water finished running out, he listened hard. Nothing. It didn't sound like Autumn's dad was inside yet.

Drying yourself was easy when the towel was thick and soft and absorbent. And the size of a city park. Cody slid into his spare shirt. He only had one pair of pants, so he got back into those. Only one pair of socks too, but he switched them so that the hole was on the baby toe of the other foot. Not too obvious.

He hung up the towel, checked himself in the mirror over the sink. The bruises were more colorful, but they didn't hurt much. Or maybe being clean made him feel better. Okay, now he'd wait for Autumn to—

A sudden burst of music grabbed his attention with both hands. It was coming from downstairs, and it was loud enough that the floor was vibrating. Cody stood in the middle of the bathroom, frozen. *What was going on?*

The music stopped as suddenly as it started. Now he could hear voices. A dad voice and Autumn. They were both talking loudly. Cody got it. Autumn was smart. She was using the music to cover up shower noise, and to warn him that her dad was inside.

The voices coming from downstairs were clear.

"Sorry, Dad. I shouldn't have played the music so loud."

"I'm sorry too. I shouldn't have snapped at you."

Cody's mouth fell open. Autumn's dad had said he was sorry. Wow. His dad had never said sorry for anything. Not even for drawing blood.

The best place to hide would be under the bed. Cody grabbed his pack, snuck through the bathroom door, and found himself *in the hall!*

Crap!

Looking over his shoulder, he realized his mistake. There were two doors in the bathroom—one to Autumn's room and one to the hall. He'd gone through the wrong door. What was it with this place? Two of everything!

Good thing the hall was empty. Or at least it was right then. But a second later, a long nose appeared at floor level from the top of the main stairway. The front stairs. Cody choked back his scream as the nose moved higher and forward, revealing a moist dark eye, a floppy ear, and a row of gleaming teeth.

It was the head of a giant hound!

* * *

Cody was scared to death of dogs. The sight of this one made him wish he had decided to sleep in the ravine the night before. He'd have been cold and hungry and dirty, but he wouldn't be spending this moment down the hall from a monster.

The great head turned. Now Cody could see both eyes and ears, and a lot more teeth. And the dog could see Cody. The mouth opened wider.

The hall filled with the sound of furious barking. Cody leaped backward into the bathroom, closing the door. Too loud! Then came Autumn's dad's voice.

"What's going on, Boomer? What's the problem?"

The dog was outside the bathroom door, scratching and barking.

Crap!

Double crap!

Great steaming mounds of double crap!

Cody dashed into Autumn's bedroom, his heart firing like a machine gun. He threw himself under the bed, dragging his backpack after him.

He heard Autumn's voice.

"What's wrong, Dad?"

"Boomer seemed pretty excited. The bathroom door isn't usually closed. Is anyone in there?"

"No! I don't know! How should I know?"

Autumn sounded like she was panicking.

"Let me check. Hel-lo!" she called in a totally false voice, knocking firmly. "Anyone in there? I'm coming in . . . Nope. No one in there."

Now she sounded relieved.

"Boomer!" called Dad. "What's wrong, boy?"

The monster's claws scratched and scrabbled on the tile floor.

"What do you smell, Boomer?"

Cody could hear it all from under the bed. The girl, the man, and the hideous dog were going to come in and find him! What to do? He knew the fight-or-flight response, but that wasn't how he felt now. Maybe they should change the name to *fight or flight . . . or throw up.*

The dog growled and scratched, making a lot of noise. Not as much as Autumn, who shouted, "Stay out of my room, Dad!"

"Boomer smells something in there. What's going on, Autumn?"

Cody shut his eyes. *Sure, that'll help*, said the sarcastic voice in his head. He clamped a hand over his mouth so he wouldn't breathe noisily.

"Do you think there's someone in there?" Autumn asked loudly. "Do you think I let a stranger into my room, Dad? Ha. Ha. Ha."

The fakest laugh Cody had ever heard.

"If there *was* someone in my room, they'd be gone by now,

eh? Run downstairs and outside while we're here in the bathroom. Yeah, that's what they'd do."

Oh no. Oh no. Oh—wait a minute, thought Cody.

"I don't want to invade your privacy, Autumn," said her dad. "You know that."

Wait. Was Autumn sending him a coded message? *Run downstairs?* Not much of a code, since she said it out loud: run downstairs and outside. She didn't say his name, but she might as well have.

"Hey, you in there!" Autumn called. "We are coming into the room. I'll count to three. Ready? One . . ."

Cody wriggled out from under the bed, pulled open the door to the hall, slipped through.

"Two . . ."

He closed the door gently and ran on tiptoe toward the back stairs.

"Three. Here we come!"

He didn't hear what happened next. He was downstairs and out the door he came in.

There was a big metal bowl on the floor over in the corner of the studio. Why hadn't he noticed it earlier? Cody shivered. He didn't want to get bitten.

Dad hated dogs. "Never let them get too close," he said once.

"They've got teeth like razors. They'll grab hold of your arm and rip it to shreds!"

Would Boomer rip Cody's arm to shreds? Maybe. He thought about leaving. He imagined himself sleeping down in the ravine, or hitchhiking to another town. No Boomer. But there might be other dogs. And . . . was he *ready* to live on his own? He had twenty dollars and a spare shirt. When he thought about it, he was incredibly lucky to be where he was.

It was Friday. No school tomorrow. Could he stay here for the weekend? Then what? Cody thought about going home, but the picture of his dad was even scarier than Boomer's teeth. Cody didn't know what he *would* do, but he knew he wouldn't go home.

There was a strong smell of fresh paint in the studio. The forest picture looked different. The shapes were the same, but not the colors. The sky was gray purple yesterday, and now it was yellowish. Autumn's dad had painted on top of the gray purple. What was that about? It still didn't look realistic.

"Don't touch!"

He whirled around. Autumn was standing in the doorway.

"My dad goes crazy if you touch what he's working on."

Cody peered past her. "Is the dog with you?"

"Dad's taking him for a walk. Don't you like Boomer?"

Cody shook his head. "I don't like dogs. And I wasn't touching the painting. I'm checking out the colors."

"So you *don't* like dogs, but you like pictures? That's weird."

Neither of them had anything to say for a moment. Then Cody remembered.

"Hey, thanks for warning me. And telling me what to do. That was pretty cool, counting down and all."

Her face brightened. "I know—wasn't that—"

"Wild! I was so—"

"I hoped you'd get the message, but I didn't want to—"

"You were really smart to—"

They both stopped talking at once.

"I should go. Dad will be back soon with Boomer."

"Thanks for checking on me," Cody said. "And thanks for the shower too. I . . ." He took a breath. "I appreciate all you're doing for me."

She started to walk away, then turned back. "I get that your dad is awful, Cody. What about your mom—could you stay with her?"

He shook his head. "She's not around."

Autumn put her hand to her mouth. "Oh, I'm so sorry. I didn't know she was—"

"No, no, no, she's not dead. She's . . . away."

"And you can't stay there?"

Cody shook his head again. Thinking about Mom made him angry. If she was still around, Dad wouldn't be picking on him. It was her fault for ending up where she did. She shouldn't have gotten caught.

"You can go out if you want," said Autumn, "but don't sleep late. Dad may be in here early. He wants this painting done by next weekend . . . Are you going to the party? I don't know if I will."

It was Friday night, so of course there was a party. And of course Autumn was invited. And of course he was not.

"I'm okay here. You go to the party. Say hi to your new boyfriend."

"What?" She turned back fully now, her mouth working like she was about to spit. "What did you say about a new boyfriend?"

"I heard it from—"

"I do not have a new boyfriend. I don't care what they say. Connor is— They're all wrong. I may not go the party at all. Mia is being a pain right now. And anyway, I promised Davros and some Daleks I'd hang out with them. If you know what I mean."

He shook his head. "No idea."

"Good." She marched out the door, slamming it shut. Then, a second later, pulled the door open again to shout in at him.

"New boyfriend—ha!"

This time she slammed the door so hard the water in the dog's dish did one of those *Jurassic Park* ripples.

AUTUMN

Autumn had a TV in her room, but she opted for curling up on the sofa in her pj's in front of the fireplace and watching *Doctor Who* on the big screen. The sound of her parents moving around the house was far better than yet another stupid party. She had devoured half a bowl of popcorn and two cans of Diet Coke before she remembered Cody outside in the dark studio all alone.

She must have shifted her position because Boomer, curled up against her leg, huffed sleepily.

"Sorry, buddy." She reached back and scratched between his ears. "What do you think he's doing out there?" she asked him.

"What do I think *who's* doing out *where*?" a voice said behind her.

"GAH!" Autumn leaped up, spilling her popcorn and sending Boomer off the couch and into a barking frenzy. "Mom!"

"Sorry. I didn't mean to scare you. Who are you talking to?"

"Boomer," Autumn admitted, shoveling handfuls of popcorn up and dumping them back into the bowl. "Are you going to bed already?"

"Yeah. Early night. I wouldn't be surprised if your dad is already snoring." She laughed. "You need anything before I head up?"

"No. I'm fine. Good night." Autumn smiled as her mom leaned down and kissed her head and then climbed the stairs to her room as Boomer whined at the back door.

At Cody. Autumn sighed.

She should probably check on him, right? Couldn't she just go to bed and let him fend for himself tonight? They weren't friends. She barely knew him. But there was something about him that made her want to help him.

She blamed her parents for that.

For as long as she could remember, they had volunteered together as a family, and her parents had always taught her how lucky they were to have a nice house and food and clothes when so many people didn't have anything. Cody didn't have a home. Or at least a *safe* home he could go back to. He was wearing dirty jeans that looked like they could stand up by themselves and socks with a hole so large his big toe stuck out.

And someone had beaten the hell out of him. His dad, from what she could gather. She tried to imagine her own father ever hitting her. Her big, gentle father who painted the most beautiful pictures. Who sobbed when Tony Stark died in *Avengers: Endgame* and who stayed up all night cuddling and singing to

Boomer when he got sprayed by a skunk and wouldn't come out from under the dining room table. He never raised his voice to her, let alone his hand.

She was lucky. And fortunate. And the kid hiding out in her dad's studio was most definitely neither of those things. Despite knowing full well her parents—kind as they were—wouldn't appreciate her harboring a strange boy in their house, and despite knowing that her friends would 100 percent cast her out of their group, she wanted to help Cody.

She wanted to help him. He looked like a skinny little puppy that had been kicked around too much.

Boomer nuzzled her hand with his wet nose.

"You're right, buddy," Autumn told him. "I bet he's hungry. Let's bring him a snack."

Boomer followed Autumn into the backyard, leaping around like a furry maniac as he checked the perimeter of the house.

"No barking, Boomer," she cautioned him. He huffed back at her. "I mean it." She was juggling a plate stacked high with a couple slices of cold pizza, a handful of Oreos, an apple, and a bottle of water in one hand. In the other, she had a pile of clean clothes that had been stacked in a hamper her dad had forgotten to bring upstairs.

She wasn't sure how she was going to let Cody know it was

her outside without freaking him out. She tapped softly at the door to the studio with the toe of her shoe. "Hey!" she hissed. "It's me." Boomer chuffed under his breath. "Yeah, yeah. You're here too." She smiled.

The door opened a crack, and Autumn saw Cody's bruised face peering out at her.

"Let me in. I brought food," she whispered. Before either of them could move, Boomer jumped at the door and pushed. "Boomer!" Under Boomer's considerable weight, the door flew open and Cody landed flat on his butt on the studio floor. Before Autumn could grab Boomer's collar, he had pinned Cody down and was enthusiastically and very happily licking his face.

"Help me!" Cody screamed. Autumn put down the plate and closed the door before anyone could hear. "Help!"

"Shhh! It's just Boomer." She grabbed his collar and tried to pull him away, but he was enjoying his new friend too much. "He's friendly. Boomer! Get off him!" Boomer was still on top of Cody, but stopped licking his face long enough to look at Autumn. "Sit! Sit down, you silly dog." Boomer sat and wagged his tail happily.

Cody was pushing himself away with his feet and wiping at his face with his arm, whimpering under his breath. Autumn felt bad, but honestly, how could anyone be afraid of a big Muppet like Boomer?

"Cody, he's friendly. I promise." She reached down and offered a hand. "I brought you some food," she told him, hauling him to his feet. He looked over her shoulder at Boomer. "Just pet him. He'll be your friend for life."

"Nah, I'm good."

Autumn shrugged. She gestured to the plate. "Hungry?"

Cody nodded, picking up a slice of pizza and taking a huge bite. "Thanks," he mumbled through a mouthful of food.

"No problem." Autumn ran her fingers through Boomer's fur. He was waiting patiently for any dropped morsels from Cody. "Throw him a piece of chicken." Cody looked at her blankly, then sighed and picked a bit of chicken off his pizza. "See? I told you he was friendly."

"Right," he said, stuffing his mouth with another bite and looking distrustfully at Boomer.

"Oh! I almost forgot. I brought you some clean clothes. I can throw your stuff in with my laundry if you want." She handed him a pair of her dad's sweatpants, an old college sweatshirt of his, and a clean pair of socks. "My dad is bigger than you, but the pants have a drawstring so they should be okay."

"Won't he miss them?" Cody asked, putting down his pizza long enough to run his hand over the soft fabric of the sweatshirt.

"He's got lots of clothes," she told him, and then instantly wished she could take the words back. Cody had two T-shirts and a pair of jeans, and she felt like she was bragging or something. "It's okay. You can borrow them. Do you have a toothbrush and toothpaste? And . . ." She blushed. "Underwear?"

Cody's face flushed. "Yeah," he stammered.

"Okay!" Autumn answered far too loudly. "Great. Why don't you change, and I'll take your dirty stuff in and wash it."

"Right here?" Cody looked around the big open space of the studio and then back at Autumn.

"I'll turn around!" she said. "Boomer! Leave it." Boomer left the piece of pizza he had been sniffing and ran to her side. She turned her back dramatically and kept up a steady stream of conversation so she didn't have to listen to him getting undressed. "You're not a vegetarian, I guess. I didn't really think of that before I grabbed the pizza. My mom is a vegetarian, but my dad still eats meat. I think I'm more of a pescatarian? Do you know what that is? It's someone who eats fish. Do you have any favorite foods? I think my favorite food is spaghetti. My dad makes awesome spaghetti."

Autumn was so busy talking she didn't see the flashlight moving across the backyard. She didn't hear the door to the studio opening or the gasp from the doorway. She didn't see her father until Boomer bounded across the room and jumped on him.

"Dad!" Autumn looked from her frowning father to Cody,

who was holding out his dirty jeans to her, his mouth moving like a fish out of water with no words coming out. "I can explain!"

Her dad looked at Cody, his head tilted to the side.

"Is that my sweatshirt?"

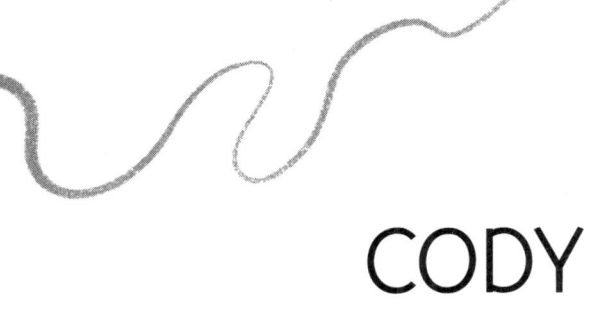

CODY

Cody's first thought was relief. If Autumn's dad had arrived one minute earlier, he—Cody—would have had no pants on.

Things were bad, but not as bad as they could be.

"It's way too big for you."

Cody couldn't trust himself to speak. He nodded.

"What about the sweats? They're mine too, right? I'm guessing those jeans are yours." He pointed.

"Dad!" said Autumn again. "I know this looks weird. I wanted to tell you, but—"

"Tell me what?"

There was an edge to the tone. The man was not happy. Cody stepped to one side so he had a clearer view of his hands. Not fists. Yet.

One of them had paint flecks on the back. And there was dirt under the nails too. They were not as big as his dad's, not as muscular, but these were working hands.

"To tell you about Cody." She turned away from her dad and gave Cody an encouraging head bob. Encouraging but frustrated too. Like: *Come on, say something!*

Cody sketched a wave. "That's me," he said.

There was a painful silence. Cody tried to explain why he was here.

"Autumn saw me on the street last night. She was on her way to a party. She stopped and, well, picked me up."

"I see," said her dad.

"You were lying on the ground," Autumn snapped. "I helped you up."

"We came back here," Cody continued. "And there was a couch."

"I see," her dad said again.

"Because you were running away from home and needed a place to sleep. That's why the couch."

"As for right now, well, I wasn't wearing any clothes—"

"I see."

"No!" Autumn threw his jeans to the floor. Unlike her father, she was clenching her fists tight. "No! Jeez, Cody. You are telling this all wrong.

Autumn's dad perched on one arm of the couch. He had a smile on his face. Not a big smile. Not a warm smile. But a smile.

"Let's be civilized about this. We'll start with names. You're Cody. I'm Tom. I like to paint. From your face, seems that you like to fight. That's Autumn over there. You know her, Cody.

Go to school together, I guess. Autumn is the girl who picked you up. That kind of thing never happened to me when I was your age, but I'm sure—"

"Dad! No! That's not how—"

"You'll get a chance to talk, Wibbly. I'm starting with our guest. Why don't you sit down, Cody? On the couch. Perfect. Here we all are on a Friday evening. You seem to be at home, Cody. My studio. My clothes. My daughter. Can I ask how long this has been going on?"

"Dad! You've got it all—"

"Shhh. What do you say, Cody?"

Cody had no idea what Autumn's dad—Tom—was talking about. How long had all *what* been going on?

"Uh, I stayed the night," he said. "Autumn let me in here late. About the clothes—well, that was her idea. But I didn't have anything to put on, and—"

"Cody!"

She had been fizzing like a shaken can of soda. Now she exploded.

"Cody, shut up! Dad, listen. There is no *all this*. Cody is *not* my boyfriend. He's not really a friend at all. He ran away from home because his own dad beat the crap out of him. That's why he looks like that. I found him on the street and took him back here. I wanted to tell you and Mom, but he begged me not to say anything in case the cops or his dad came and dragged him back. I'm sorry. I didn't know what to do."

She spoke loudly enough to startle Boomer. He lifted his head. Cody was startled too. His mouth fell open in surprise. Was *this* what they were talking about? Him and Autumn? Wow. Cody had never thought about her that way. She was cool. She wouldn't have anything to do with him. He hadn't thought about dating pop stars either, or models on magazine covers.

Mr. . . . Tom . . . Autumn's dad was looking at Cody now. He had great eyebrows—dark and wriggly, like caterpillars. One of them quirked up.

"That right? Do you have anything to add?" he asked.

Cody shook his head.

"I'm glad," said Autumn, "that you found out, Dad. I don't like having secrets."

The smile was warmer now. You could tell he meant it. "You don't have to apologize, Wibbly. I was wrong. I just assumed a few things when I saw Cody here in my sweatshirt."

"I'm wearing your pants too. They're big, but there's a drawstring."

Neither Autumn nor her dad looked at him.

"I'm glad to know what's going on. It's better this way. I'm sorry I didn't let you talk earlier."

"Hey, that's the second time today you said sorry. You said it in the bathroom too. Remember? I heard you. I was hiding in Autumn's room."

The eyebrows came down in a dark hairy V.

V.

Like that.

"What?" he growled from deep in his throat, staring intently at Cody.

Off to the side, Autumn was shaking her head at him, waving with her hands like an umpire calling safe.

Oh, right. Cody talked without thinking sometimes. This was one of them.

"Nothing," he muttered. "Nothing at *aaaaah*—!"

The sudden scream was because Boomer had climbed onto the couch beside him. The dog yawned wide enough to swallow a cantaloupe, put his head on Cody's rigid thigh, and sighed happily.

Autumn's dad was still looking pretty fierce. But—this was a funny thing—Cody did not think he was going to hit him. It was more than just the hands. It was the way he apologized. It was the way he and Autumn *were* together.

The moment stretched. Cody was aware of the dog not biting him. He was aware of Autumn's dad not hitting him. At least not yet.

Autumn was standing by the paint-spattered table in the

middle of the room. She put the question that Cody was afraid to ask.

"What are you going to do, Dad?"

"I don't know. Maybe your mom will have an answer."

"NO! Don't tell!" Cody jumped to his feet, disturbing the dog. "Don't tell anyone. Don't—just don't. I won't go back home. I won't do it. I'll leave now."

He looked around wildly. Where was his backpack? Behind the couch? By the door? Where was it? He took a big step and almost bumped into Autumn's dad, who had risen to his feet.

"Out of the way, sir! Please! I won't . . ." Cody ran out of steam because of what he could see in the man's face. Something he had never seen in his own father's face. The last thing he expected from a father.

Pain. Sympathy. Pity.

"Listen, Cody." The deep voice was gentle now. "Listen to me. You won't go back to a place where you get beaten. That will not happen. I won't let it, and neither will my wife. Autumn may have broken some rules to sneak you in here. But she did the right thing. Take a deep breath. Sit back on the couch. Okay?"

Cody couldn't speak. He was trying to process a lot at once. He sat down.

"Good. Stay there while I explain the situation to my wife. She's a doctor. She'll want to examine you. Then we'll work out what happens next. Autumn, pass me those jeans. What about Cody's shirt? Might as well wash everything. Then I can have my sweats back."

He took the dirty clothes and left the studio.

Autumn and Cody stared at each other. Her face was scrunched up. Cody couldn't tell if she was happy or mad or relieved. Maybe all three. He wanted to say something nice, but he couldn't find the words. *Your dad is amazing* sounded stupid.

He remembered the nickname her dad called her.

"Wibbly?" he said. "What's that?"

"Nothing. Shut up."

"Is it your middle name? Something you said when you were a baby?"

"Shut up!"

She was sort of mad now. Was she relieved too?

Cody's hand felt wet. He looked down, startled. Boomer was licking him.

AUTUMN

Wibbly. He hadn't called her that in a while. Not since the time he had blurted out the old nickname in front of her friends and she thought she was going to die of embarrassment. Literally die. The sound of Mia and Aliyah choking with laughter made her face burn even now. She had snapped at her dad and regretted it the instant his face fell.

"WIBBLY?" Mia had shrieked the second he was out of the room. "What the heck is a wibbly?" She leaned against Aliyah for support, laughing with her mouth open so wide Autumn could see her back teeth.

Like a horse, she thought meanly.

She felt bad. Briefly. Before Mia started braying, "Wibbly! Come here, Wibbly. Little Wibbly Wobbly Autumn with her Wibbly Wobbly bottom."

What did that even mean? Was it a butt joke? It didn't matter. Mia was supposed to be her friend, but she jumped at any chance to make herself look better than everyone else.

Autumn had laughed along because it was easier than getting upset. Connor changed the subject smoothly and everyone started throwing around ideas for the science project while Mia and Aliyah snickered at her behind their hands.

Wibbly. A *Doctor Who* reference that none of her friends got. As in, "Wibbly wobbly, timey wimey stuff."

She wasn't about to explain any of that to this kid who had never heard of the Doctor and would think she was a total loser for liking it as much as she did.

She glanced up at Cody. He was leaning away from Boomer, who had draped his massive furry frame over him and rested his head in his lap.

"He likes you," she said.

Cody looked up from the corner of the sofa he had wedged himself into.

"He does?"

Boomer took advantage of Cody's distraction to lick the entire side of his face. "GAH!" Cody screamed.

"Stop thrashing around and he'll settle down. Jeez. How can you possibly be afraid of Boomer? He's a Muppet."

Boomer wagged his tail happily at Autumn, who sat in front of the sofa and rubbed his soft ears.

She grabbed his collar and pulled gently, but he shook her off and settled his big head back in Cody's lap.

"Dude! He's afraid of you. Come on." Boomer closed his eyes and ignored her completely. Within seconds he was snoring gently. "Umm. I'm sorry. I think he really likes you."

Cody stared down at the giant mop sleeping on top of him. "It's fine. I guess. I mean, he won't bite me or anything, right?"

Autumn laughed and then realized Cody was only sort of kidding. "Boomer has never bitten anyone in his life. He's more likely to lick you to death. I promise. He's a good dog." Boomer's ears perked up. "You big faker! Boomer, get off him right now!"

Even Cody cracked a smile when Boomer bounded off him to land like a discarded mop on Autumn, knocking her over.

Autumn stood up and walked over to the door. Cody was still pressed into the corner of the sofa.

"You coming?" she asked. Her dad clearly wanted to feed him, and her mom was going to want to meet him. She may as well bring him in before they both came out looking for them.

"Are you sure?" Cody asked.

"Am I sure about what?"

"That I should come in?"

"My dad was serious. He's in there telling my mom about you right now. And he'll want to feed you. Just come in before they both come out here. At least you'll get something more to eat while they're talking."

She turned and headed outside with Boomer. After a few

steps, she heard Cody coming out behind her and following her across the yard.

"Welcome to our home, Cody." Autumn's mom held the door for him and waved them into the house. "My husband is just whipping up something for you to eat. Autumn, why don't you show him where the powder room is?"

"Sure. It's the third door to the left. The kitchen is at the end of the hall." Cody was looking around like he'd never been inside a house before. It was pretty unnerving. But then, Autumn *had* found him sleeping under a bush, so . . .

Cody trudged past them and went into the powder room. Autumn turned to her mom, knowing she probably had a million questions.

"His father is going to wonder where he is, Autumn," her mom whispered. "The police could be looking for him if he's a runaway."

"Well, you saw his face. He can't go back home."

"How well do you know this boy?" her mother asked.

"I met him yesterday. I knew *of* him. But we don't exactly hang out with the same people." She led the way to the kitchen, where her father was pulling a plate heaped high with steaming leftovers out of the microwave.

"I hope this is okay," he called out to Cody, who was lurking in the doorway.

"Yeah," Cody mumbled, slinking into the kitchen and sitting in the chair Autumn's mom had pulled out for him. "Thanks, Mr. . . . uhhh . . ." Cody was clearly realizing he had no idea what Autumn's last name was, and his face turned bright red. It was almost funny.

"Bird."

"Huh?" Cody looked confused.

"Our last name. It's Bird," Autumn told him. Cody gaped at her.

"Your real name is Autumn Bird?" He smirked. Autumn shot a death glare at him. She liked her name, and this puny little kid wasn't going to make fun of her for it. Not in her own house!

"Yes. It is. I was born in the fall, and Bird is a common name where my parents are from." She frowned at him. "I know your last name is Stouffer because I hear it at school. *Cody Stouffer, report to the office.*"

Her father cleared his throat.

Cody looked over at him, then down at the plate in front of him.

"Thanks, Mr. . . . ummm . . . Bird. Mr. Bird."

"You're welcome." Her dad smiled. "We're going to let you eat, Cody Stouffer. Then my wife will be back to take a look at your face and maybe we can sit down and figure out a game plan. Sound good?"

"Umm. Yeah. Yes. Thank you."

"Great. Autumn will keep you company."

Autumn opened her mouth to protest but closed it when she caught the look on her dad's face. Fine. She'd babysit him for a few minutes. Cody was already stuffing his face before her parents had left the room. Autumn wrinkled her nose at the chomping noises and looked away.

"Did your dad paint all the stuff on the walls?" he asked, his mouth full of meat loaf and mashed potatoes.

"What? Oh. Yeah."

"It's cool." Autumn watched wordlessly as he stuffed another forkful of food into his mouth. "Like Indian stuff or whatever," he continued.

"Indian stuff?" Autumn snapped. "Are you serious?"

"Like that one of the guy in the fancy costume?" Cody was oblivious.

"That's my uncle," she told him through clenched teeth. "And it's not a costume. He's wearing regalia."

Cody glanced up at her.

"Oh. Well . . . so you're an Indian?" he asked.

"We're Cree." Autumn was clenching her fists so tightly her nails were digging into her palms.

"Isn't that the same thing?"

"We're Indigenous," she hissed.

"So?" Dad asked from the doorway. "What are we talking about?"

CODY

Cody felt lighter. Why? It took him a second to work it out. Then he got it. He was relieved.

Ever since Autumn had picked him up and found him a place to stay, Cody had felt bothered. It was no fun being grateful. But that was only part of it. Autumn had so much more going for her than he did. Cody couldn't help comparing her place to his, her parents to his, her life to his. She was just—well—*better* than him. There was no way to keep up with her. But now the pressure was off. They were not the same, him and her. The relief made Cody feel friendly.

"Oh, hi," he said to her dad with a smile. "We weren't talking about anything important."

"We were talking about backgrounds," said Autumn, very tight-lipped. "Cody is surprised that our family is Indigenous."

"No, no. I mean, that's your uncle with feathers and war paint." Cody pointed toward the picture. "It's not much of a surprise that you guys are . . . Indigenous. Do you happen to know a guy named Joe? He works with my dad sometimes. A construction guy. My dad calls him the crazy Indian."

Autumn let out her breath in a *pah* of disgust. Her dad showed no reaction. There was no expression on his face. None at all.

Cody could see he'd made a mistake, but he didn't know what.

"I don't mean to make fun," he said. "Crazy is his nickname. I'm sure he's not crazy—but he acts weird sometimes and, well, being an Indian . . . So I guess you don't know Joe. I just wondered, being . . . you know . . . like him, that you might know him. That's all."

Neither of them responded for a few seconds. Then Autumn opened her mouth.

"Dad, can I please kick him?"

Now the man reacted. Not to Cody. He turned and he chuckled appreciatively at his daughter's question.

"Please, Dad. You said I could always stand up to a bully. Remember? You said I didn't have to put up with anything nasty and mean."

"Cody is a guest here."

"Come on, Dad. Let me kick him just once. He deserves it."

Still laughing, he answered, "I suppose he does. But Cody is not worth kicking, Wibbly. Look at his poor face. He ran away from home, and home is where he got his ideas. He doesn't know any better yet. But you do."

What were they talking about? Cody didn't understand. He

must have stepped over some weird family line here. Funny about Autumn—now that he knew the dude in the picture was her uncle, he could see the resemblance.

"You are being *such* a dork," she said. "What's with you?" She looked mad enough to explode.

"Are you finished eating, Cody?" her dad asked. "Your plate is empty. Do you want any more?"

"No, I'm good."

"I don't know that I'd agree with that. But you're full. So let's go and see the doctor."

"Doctor? You said your wife would take a look at me."

"My wife is a doctor."

"Oh. Yeah, that's right."

Cody got up from the table. With a last look at the picture of Autumn's uncle, he followed her dad out of the kitchen.

The hallway was old stone tiles, polished until they shone. The ceiling was way high, with a fancy light fixture hanging down. Everything smelled fresh and flowery and sort of rich. Was rich a smell? Cody liked it.

They went past a staircase and down another hall. Mr. Bird was a few steps ahead. They passed a picture with a single small light shining down on it. Cody stopped. Mr. Bird kept going for a few steps, then realized he was alone and turned around.

Cody was staring.

It was a lot like the picture in the studio. Rocks, water, a tree, a cloudy sky. It was good. It was really good. Cody felt like he could walk into it. And yet it wasn't like a photograph. There was odd blurring around the edges of the shapes. It made the space bigger. This small forest scene looked like, like, a stadium. Or a cathedral. Something like that.

How did he do it? He. *T. Bird*. The name at the bottom of the picture.

He. Autumn's dad, who had walked back to see what was going on. All his movements were slow, calm, confident. Maybe his confidence came from being so big. But there was more to it than size. It was like he was confident from the inside out. Cody wanted to ask him something, but couldn't find the words. Which made sense because he didn't really know what he wanted to ask.

"How did you . . ." he began. But he couldn't finish.

"How did . . ." But that question died too. It was about the picture.

"How—" Cody still couldn't find the words.

"You're not laughing," Mr. Bird said.

"No. I . . . It's . . . the picture. I . . . wow. That's all." Cody waved his hands.

"Oh! You like it? At first I thought you were making a *Lone Ranger* joke with all those *how*s. You think it's the way we all talk. It's easy to laugh at a crazy Indian. You said so."

Cody had been feeling pretty comfy a minute ago. Now he was confused. It was like he was being rained on from a clear blue sky. Where was the rain coming from? Autumn and her dad were mad at him, and he didn't know why.

Dad did the same thing—got mad because of something Cody said. But these guys were not like his dad. Autumn didn't have to help him, but she did. Her dad called Cody a guest. If they were mad at him, he deserved it. He'd said something bad. He just didn't know what it was.

"Anything to add, Cody?"

Cody shook his head. Tom—Mr. Bird—sighed.

"Well, I'm glad you like the picture. We're going to my wife's office. You can call her Dr. Bird. Okay?"

Cody nodded. Mr. Bird knocked on the door and waited. Which was weird, right? It was his house. Cody's dad never knocked on doors.

When they went in, Autumn's mom was sitting at a computer, typing. She got to her feet. Mr. Bird led Cody in and disappeared.

The examination was fast. Dr. Bird was a birdlike woman who bustled around Cody, cleaning his face with warm water she got from a sink—yes, there was a sink in the office!—then tapping his chest and back, staring into his eyes, and asking him how he was feeling. Then she asked what day of the week it was and who was the prime minister. When he said he had no idea, she gave a quick nod and asked him who won the Stanley Cup last year.

"I don't know—the Maple Leafs?" It was a guess. Everyone talked about the Maple Leafs. The only other hockey name Cody could remember was Wayne what's-his-name. And that was only because his dad yelled at Wayne all the time. He didn't like him.

"If you're a friend of my daughter's, you must know what Doctor Who travels in. What is that called?"

He looked at her blankly. She raised her hands in an *I give up* gesture.

"So much for general knowledge. How many fingers am I holding up?"

"Uhhh, three."

Dr. Bird had dark eyes and black hair. Her nose had a bend at the top. Her skin was a little darker than Autumn's. She would fit into an old movie with cowboys, except that she talked fast—way faster than her husband or any of those TV Indians. She told him to sit in a chair, then perched on the edge of her desk to talk to him.

"The good news is that you are healthy. Your bruises are

progressing nicely. Your brain function seems"—she smiled to herself like she was making a joke—"unaffected. You are experiencing pain, so I'm going to suggest ibuprofen. Autumn will give you some. But you are an otherwise healthy young man, and you should recover in a few days."

He didn't know what to say, so she went on. "I understand that you ran away from home because of your father's ill treatment. I am very sorry you had to deal with that. You are still a minor, so I have some reporting obligations as a doctor. May I ask what your plans are?"

"My plans?" he said. "What plans?"

"Look, Cody, let's keep this simple. You ran away from home. Are you headed anywhere in particular?"

"No."

"What would you have done if Autumn had not found you? Slept on the street?"

"I guess so."

"For how long?"

"I don't know—until I got a job."

"You're, what, thirteen? Fourteen? It's hard to find any job at that age, let alone one that will support you."

There was a funny scratching sound from behind him. He turned. There it was again. Dr. Bird walked past him to the door of her office.

"Autumn says your mother is not available. Is there anyone else you can stay with?" She opened the door, and the big dog came charging in. It must have been him scratching. The dog ran to Cody's chair, stopped, and looked up.

Boomer, that was the dog's name.

"Hey, Boomer." Cody reached down and very, very, *very* gently patted the dog's head. Boomer licked his hand. He seemed to like licking Cody's hand. He did it in the studio too. Cody patted a little harder.

"Well, well," said Dr. Bird. "There's *someone* who wants you. Too bad Boomer doesn't have a house of his own, or you could stay with him."

Was she joking? Not about Boomer, but was she telling Cody that he couldn't keep on staying there? Maybe she was.

Cody's mind was a mess. The weight on his shoulders was back. He didn't know how he felt about anyone. Autumn was generous yesterday, and now she was angry. Her dad was cool, but he didn't seem to like Cody talking about Crazy Joe. Now Autumn's mom was talking about him living on the street. Who were these people really?

What was the thing his dad always said about Joe—*You just can't trust them,* he said. Meaning Indians. Could that be true? Boomer might be the only one he could count on.

"I have one more tough question for you," said Dr. Bird. "I

hate things hanging on. We should clear this up quickly."

She stepped into the hall.

"Tom!" she called. "Come here, please!"

Cody was afraid. He knew what was about to happen. Dr. and Mr. Bird were going to throw him out into the street. He'd have to remember to get his jeans and shirt from Autumn—he couldn't wear Mr. Bird's clothes when he was on his own. At least they'd be clean. And he had a full stomach.

Mr. Bird came into the room. Cody got to his feet. Time to go. But the doctor didn't dismiss him yet.

"You know what we talked about earlier, Tom?" she said. "Now that I've seen Cody, I think we have to try."

Mr. Bird nodded. "I'll take him," he said. "When—tonight?"

"Right now."

Take him where? Were they going to ride him out of their nice neighborhood? Or all the way out of town? Maybe that was it. They were going to dump him at the end of the subway line.

"I need my clothes and backpack," said Cody. "And I should say goodbye to Autumn."

He knew he should thank the Birds for feeding him, and for giving him a place to sleep. But he was upset. And a little mad. Dr. Bird was at her computer.

"You won't need your backpack, Cody," she said.

"What, you're going to kick me out with nothing? I didn't have much—just that backpack."

"We're not kicking you out," said Autumn's dad. "Why would we kick you out? You're a guest."

"But I—"

"You got beat up. Mary is writing a report now. It's the law. You and I are going to visit your dad now and tell him."

Cody shrank back. "No," he whispered.

"Yes."

Cody's mouth opened wide enough to swallow a car. He yelled. Not a shriek or a cry; the sound was more like a car horn or foghorn, or a siren, or a dog baying at the moon.

"Awooooooooooo!" is what it sounded like.

And, right on cue, Boomer raised his head and gave tongue. The two cries echoed off the walls of the office, making the chandelier tinkle. They spread throughout the house, loud, urgent, eerily similar in timbre. "Awooooooooooo! Awooooooooooo!"

Cody shrank to the floor, and Boomer started licking his face. The silence was deafening.

AUTUMN

Autumn was fuming. Pacing around her room, absolutely fuming. She had let that kid stay in her dad's studio, fed him, gotten him clean clothes, LIED TO HER PARENTS, and he had basically sat there, looking them in the eyes and calling them stupid Indians.

It just figured.

Her parents were constantly telling her things like *don't judge a book by its cover* and *treat others the way you want to be treated*, and she tried. She really did. But this kid made her so mad with his stupid, racist words and his dumb face lurching around her house. Her parents might think they should be generous and kind, but Cody didn't deserve it. He made it feel like the air was being sucked out of the entire house. Autumn took a deep breath, but it didn't calm her down. If anything, it made her even madder.

"I have to get out of here." she muttered under her breath.

She threw a hoodie over her Spider-Man pj's and left her room, nearly tripping over Boomer's giant stuffed dog that he'd left spread across her doorway like a big floppy rug.

She smiled and stepped over it and headed down the stairs.

Her mom looked up from her favorite reading chair, where she was sipping a cup of tea and reading some British thriller.

"Where are you going, Autumn? It's getting kind of late."

"I know. I'm just running down the street to Mia's for a second. I won't be long."

"All right. Half an hour. Then straight home, okay?"

"Okay . . . Mom?"

"Hmmhm?"

"Does he really have to stay here? After all the things he said about us?" Autumn felt her eyes prickling and rubbed at them angrily.

Her mom took her reading glasses off and put them down with her book on the side table.

"Autumn, come over here." She took Autumn's hands in hers. "I know that Cody said some really hurtful things. And I know you must be angry."

"I am!" Autumn agreed.

"It made me angry too. But it also made me sad."

"Sad? Why?" Autumn asked.

"Because Cody doesn't come from a happy home like you do, Autumn. He didn't have someone teaching him that everyone is equal or that we have to treat people . . ."

"The way we want to be treated," Autumn finished. Her mom nodded.

"Right. Look at him, sweetheart. He doesn't have a safe place to live. He hasn't had a loving family to teach him how to behave appropriately."

"I don't think it should be our responsibility to teach people like him why being racist is wrong," Autumn insisted.

"No. But it *is* our job to be kind. And maybe by being kind to someone who you don't think deserves it, it'll help him learn something about being kind himself."

Autumn thought about what her mother had said on the five-minute walk to Mia's house. And she remembered how she had felt when she found Cody beaten and passed out behind the hedge. She didn't like him. But she did feel bad for him. So she'd try.

Mia's mom opened the door holding a glass of wine and smiling widely, while a group of grown-ups laughed together in the background.

"They're upstairs, hon." She kissed Autumn on the cheek, a gesture Autumn never did feel comfortable with.

"Okay, thanks," she said, trying not to wipe at the lipstick mark she was absolutely positive was now on her face.

She climbed the stairs to Mia's room and had her hand on the doorknob before it registered that Mia's mom had said "they" were upstairs. Aliyah must be sleeping over. Good! She was dying to tell the girls what had been going on.

"Guys, you're not going to *believe* what I have been dealing with . . ." she said, turning the knob and stepping into Mia's room before the words died on her lips.

Connor and Mia leaped apart, but not before Autumn had seen them sitting on the bed, pressed against each other.

Kissing.

Without a word, Autumn turned and flew down the stairs toward the front door. She was outside and across the yard in seconds as Mia's voice called out behind her.

"Autumn! It was nothing!"

CODY

Cody was in the car with Mr. Bird and Boomer. The dog seemed happy, lounging across the back seat with his tongue out. He was the only one. Mr. Bird wasn't happy. He hadn't spoken since they'd left the house. Cody, sitting next to him, was far from happy. He was on his way back to his old place. His dad's place.

The sun had just gone down. This was the first layer of darkness. Not dead of night. Not quite black. If you took a black sheet of paper and rubbed a layer of gray crayon on top, it might look like this.

They were waiting for the light at Parliament and Bloor. The late spring sun was setting pink and deep orangey off to the right, behind the thin dark tower blocks of midtown. Looking left, down Parliament Street, Cody could see his building. Tall and dingy and scary.

"You won't—" he started. Meaning, *You won't hand me over to my dad?* He'd asked this before they left the house, and Mr. Bird had said no.

Mr. Bird said it again. But he didn't know how angry Dad

got, how violent, how unpredictable. And did Mr. Bird's no really mean no? Cody had heard his dad say over and over again that you couldn't trust an Indian. Look at Autumn. She took him off the street and let him into her home—and then got mad at him for nothing! Maybe her dad was lying. Maybe he did plan to hand Cody over.

The light changed. Mr. Bird made a left turn and headed down Parliament Street. The car had soft seats and clean windows and a fresh smell. It was the nicest car Cody had ever sat in. But he wasn't enjoying himself. His stomach churned like a washing machine. Cemetery on the left, bus crawling ahead of them.

"Is that the building, Cody?" Pointing.

"Yeah."

They turned into the visitors parking lot. Cody checked Autumn's dad carefully. Was he going to go back on his promise? Was he going to hand Cody over to his dad? Was he?

He might.

Cody couldn't risk it. Couldn't risk going back. He made a plan.

"Are pets allowed in the building, Cody?"

"Huh? Oh. Yeah. Yeah, they are."

Mr. Bird put a leash on Boomer and gestured for Cody to

lead the way. He opened the outer door, crossed the lobby to push the elevator call button, and waited.

The place smelled like dirt, grease, garbage, curry, laundry. Normal, in other words. Cody was more aware of the atmosphere than usual, after Autumn's place.

The elevator doors opened slooowly. Cody stood to one side, then followed Mr. Bird and Boomer and pressed the button for the top floor. The three of them were alone in the car. No one took the elevator except real oldies and those who lived high up. Cody rarely took it. Mr. Bird stood patiently. Boomer lay down facing away from the door, his big toothy mouth open like an oven as he yawned. Cody tensed his muscles.

The door scraped slooowly across the opening with its usual hitch in the middle. Cody counted down: six, five, four . . . pause . . . three, two—

At the last second, he darted through the narrow opening and ran across the lobby.

This was his plan. He'd pressed the button for the top floor so that Mr. Bird would be stuck on the elevator while it climbed and descended slooowly. Meanwhile, Cody would be running.

He wouldn't let Autumn's dad betray him and drag him back home to his own dad, to be kicked and beaten. Better to run than get fooled. Cody would head down to the ravine and the covering darkness. And then—somewhere else. Freedom. It was spring. It wouldn't get cold for months and months. By then Cody could be in California or, or, or South America.

He almost ran over his old neighbor, Mr. Ahmad from 316, at the front door. Mrs. Ahmad might have been okay, but her husband was a pain. He yelled as Cody brushed by. *Punk* was his word for Cody. He used it now.

Cody burst onto the front walk of the building, then turned to yell his father's word for Mr. Ahmad back at him. Cody didn't look where he was going and tripped over the loose flagstone in the front walk. He went sprawling.

"Score for the towelheads." Mr. Ahmad laughed. "Towelheads one, punks zero."

He stopped laughing to thank someone for holding the door for him, then went inside the building.

Cody levered himself up to his hands and knees, and stopped. Boomer's face was within licking distance of his own. The leash trailed behind.

So much for Cody's plan.

Mr. Bird stood in the doorway, leaning forward, talking to Mr. Ahmad. He waved goodbye and came over to where Cody was sitting.

"Better get up," he said.

Boomer was licking away Cody's tears.

"Come on, son." Mr. Bird pulled Cody to his feet with ease. They walked into the building together. The front door was wedged open. Mr. Bird pushed the wedge to the side.

"Your neighbor says you live in three-twelve. Is that right?" he asked. Cody nodded. "Might as well take the stairs. It's not too far. And Boomer won't get his tail caught in the elevator door so it won't close."

That's how they got out so fast. The elevator door was still partly open. The call button was flashing, like it did when the elevator wasn't working.

Boomer's nails click-clicked on the concrete steps. The stairway smelled worse than the lobby. Mr. Bird didn't seem to notice.

"Are you afraid of your dad? That makes sense. Are you afraid of anything else?"

Cody didn't answer.

"You don't trust me, do you? What do you think I'm going to do?"

Cody didn't answer.

When they got to the third floor, Mr. Bird handed him the leash.

"Hold on to Boomer, okay? Stay close to me."

Cody nodded. He was not making another plan to run away. Plans took hope and energy. Rebellion of any kind took hope and energy. Cody was out of both of these things. He was doing what he was told. It was easier.

There was a piece of paper taped to the door of 312. An official piece of paper, with a coat of arms and date stamp and a big black signature.

Cody was too scared and upset to read. The words on the paper were a blur to him.

Mr. Bird nodded at it. "Your neighbor told me about this," he said. "Your dad must have known it was coming. That may be why he was so angry. Why he beat you up so bad. Could he still be inside?"

He knocked on the door. No answer. He knocked again, harder.

Cody stared at the door. His door, apartment 312. The eviction notice was taped to it. *Multiple warnings... Final notice... City of Toronto...*

"Let's think," said Mr. Bird. "It looks like a final notice was issued two weeks ago. This one was stamped today. That lock looks brighter than the rest of the door handle. I bet they changed it. Do you have your key?"

Cody checked the small pocket in the right front of his jeans. His key pocket. Wordlessly he tried it in the lock. It didn't fit.

"So he's not there," said Mr. Bird with a sigh. "But I have to talk to him. I have to talk to someone about you. Do you have any idea where he could be? A bar? A friend's place?"

Cody shook his head.

Things were moving fast. His dad was gone. He had no home. He wasn't sad. But he was . . . something.

Walking back downstairs, Mr. Bird spoke a few words in a language Cody didn't understand. They sounded serious, echoing in the stairwell.

"What was that?"

"Something my mother used to say to me."

"Oh. Right." What did Autumn say she was—Cree? In old Western movies, everyone spoke English, but of course they'd have their own language.

Heading back to Autumn's house, the dog lolling in the back seat, Cody asked why.

"Why do you have to talk to someone about me?"

Mr. Bird hit the steering wheel hard enough to honk the horn. They were stopped at the lights at Castle Frank. The woman in the next car stared.

"Why? Because you're a child, and people should know where you are. I can't believe your dad. Walking away without looking for you. Someone should care about you!"

His voice was raw. He was upset. Boomer heard it too. The dog's head came up, and he gave a questioning whimper.

Cody reached back to pat the dog. Cody knew Mr. Bird was angry, but not angry with him. Earlier, when he was angry with Cody, he'd been calm.

"Mom used to care, a little," he said. The light changed to green. Mr. Bird grunted as he swung into the left turn.

"Used to. Is she dead? I'm sorry."

"No."

They parked under the overhang at the side of the house. Mr. Bird turned off the engine. They got out. Cody didn't know what was going to happen to him now. If Mr. Bird betrayed him, it wouldn't be to Dad. And he might not betray him at all.

Cody was too tired to make another plan to run away. He'd go where they told him. It was easier. He closed his eyes. His lips moved.

"What did you just say?"

"Huh? Nothing."

"I heard you say, *Give me strength*. Did you?"

Cody shrugged. "It's something my mom used to say." Usually after an argument with Dad. He'd stomp off and slam the door, and she'd shake her head. She never seemed to get much strength, though.

"Are you sure you're not part Cree?"

"Huh?"

"My mom says the same thing as yours." He repeated what

he'd said back in the stairwell. "That's part of a Cree prayer. *Give me the strength to walk the earth.*"

Mr. Bird put a hand on Cody's shoulder. Not to push him in any direction—just to be there. "You want a snack? Want to watch TV?"

"No, thanks."

"Okay. Let yourself into the studio and get some rest then. See you in the morning." Mr. Bird started to walk toward the house.

Cody called after him. "My mom doesn't know any Cree."

"She knows some."

AUTUMN

Autumn ran like someone was chasing her, but neither Connor nor Mia came after her. She ran around the block and away from the house, not wanting to go home. Not wanting to stop and think about what she had just seen.

She pumped her arms and ran faster and farther away from the two people she had trusted. She ran until all she could hear was her heart pounding and her feet slapping the pavement. She ran until her lungs ached and she got a stitch in her side, then she turned and headed back toward her house.

Autumn was shaking when she got home. She felt sick. Like she was going to throw up. She tried to fit her key into the lock but her hands were trembling so badly she couldn't make it work.

"Darn it!" she hissed as her key skipped over the lock for the third time.

The door opened suddenly.

Her mother stood there, bathed in the warm light from the hallway behind her.

"Autumn?"

That's all it took. Autumn burst into tears and threw herself into her mother's arms.

"Autumn, what is it?" Her mother backtracked down the hall and into the living room, holding Autumn tightly as she moved. She pulled her down onto the sofa and stroked her hair, murmuring softly that everything was going to be all right until Autumn's tears slowed to hiccups as she caught her breath.

Autumn sat up, rubbing her eyes with her sleeve and reaching for a tissue. She blew her nose with a loud *honk*.

"Sorry. I think I snotted on you." She sniffed.

Her mom shrugged. "You've gotten worse on me." She smiled gently. "Do you want to talk about it?"

Autumn thought about it.

On one hand, she didn't. She wanted to never talk about the sight of Connor and Mia kissing on Mia's bed so she could forget it ever happened. She could go back to school in one of her best Mia-approved outfits and sit with her friends and laugh at the boys and pick at her baggie of baby carrots and bottle of water the way Mia and Aliyah did.

Or she could tell her mom that the boy she was pretty sure she didn't even like—at least not as a boyfriend—cheated on her with her best friend—who wasn't much of a friend when you thought about it—and she could find a new place to sit at lunch, wear the clothes she actually liked for a change, and pack a ham-and-cheese sandwich and some freakin' Oreos!

She took a deep breath and made her choice.

"I walked in on Mia and Connor kissing," she told her mom.

"Oh." Her mom frowned. "Wow. You must have felt really hurt."

"Yeah," Autumn agreed, but that wasn't really it. "Well, maybe not hurt. I was surprised. Definitely. I didn't know they liked each other, obviously. But I'm not even sure I like him. And she hasn't really been much of a friend, so I'm not even *that* surprised. I think it just kind of proved that maybe I made a mistake."

"How so?"

"I think I chose the wrong people to be friends with," Autumn admitted. Her mother raised an eyebrow at her but didn't say anything. "Yeah. I mean, I came back to school this year and suddenly the popular kids were asking me to hang out with them. I got invited to parties that weren't for the kids from the cross-country team or the drama or film club. I got to sit at the cool table and go shopping for cool clothes and the cutest boy in school liked me!"

"I always thought you were cool," her mom told her.

"You're my mom. You have to think that." Autumn offered a watery smile.

"Maybe. But let me ask you something. Did you *like* doing all those things? Shopping for clothes and going to parties?"

"Sometimes," Autumn said.

"Okay. But did you like hanging out with Connor?"

Autumn frowned. "Not really. He's okay. But he thinks running is stupid and that Doctor Who is a vet for owls."

Autumn's mom laughed at that, and hearing herself say it out loud made Autumn feel better. Yeah, it sucked that her friend and her boyfriend had gone behind her back. But when it came down to it, she couldn't bring herself to care too much.

"Did you enjoy the same things as Mia? Or Aliyah?"

Autumn thought about the weekends when she wanted to be at a track event, but she had quit the team that year when the popular kids started asking her to hang out. She thought about the evenings she wanted to be home with Boomer watching movies and eating popcorn. She thought about the parties she hated and all the lunch periods she had spent watching the boys slurping down fries smothered in ketchup while the girls picked at salad.

"No. Not really. And they're not actually very nice to people. Not even to each other! They talk about everyone behind their backs, and they're just as bad to each other's faces."

"Then why hang out with them?" her mom asked like she already knew the answer.

So did Autumn.

"Because they were popular," she admitted. "And none of

those kids had ever even looked at me before. But I stopped hanging out with the girls from the team and I skipped doing the play this year. I don't even go to the community center every weekend anymore."

When she thought about the friends she had basically ignored this year and the stuff she had missed out on, Autumn was ashamed. Because she had become exactly the same as Mia and Aliyah and the rest of the kids who sat at the popular table.

And when it came down to it, she missed her friends. Her REAL friends. The ones she had left behind when she started worrying about what Mia thought.

"I think maybe I have some people to apologize to," she said. "And if you're going to volunteer at the center tomorrow, I'd like to come."

"I'm sure everyone would love to see you." Her mom hugged her hard.

Autumn hugged her back and then went upstairs to choose an outfit for tomorrow. She looked through her closet, pushing clothes out of the way to get to the shelves at the side where she kept the stuff she only wore when she was home alone.

She pulled out a pair of comfy jeans she had picked up at the thrift shop last year and a hoodie that said BOOK NERD.

Autumn Bird was back.

CODY

Cody ran across a field, sweat pouring down his face and his arms. He was running away from a thick black cloud. The cloud rolled toward him. Lightning zigzagged down. There was a crash of thunder. Cody dodged in time.

Wait—you can't dodge faster than lightning.

Not in real life. But this was a dream.

On the other side of the field was a forest. Cody would be safe there. He kept running, looking over his shoulder at the cloud. He stopped short. There was a deep, muddy ditch at the edge of the field. It was too wide to jump. Cody couldn't get to the forest because the ditch was in the way.

Two people appeared like magic from the trees. They were Autumn and her dad, and they looked like movie Indians. Leather clothes, headbands with black and white feathers in them.

They walked to their side of the ditch. They were directly across from Cody. They held out their hands.

Lightning struck. Cody dodged out of the way. Autumn made a *come on* gesture. Her dad leaned forward. Cody knew that his only chance was to trust them, to leap and hope they caught him.

Thunder *CRASHED!* Cody opened his eyes.

Mr. Bird was standing next to him with a tray in his hand.

"Did I wake you? Sorry. I knocked over a can of turpentine when I walked in. There's juice and toast and peanut butter. I don't know what you eat. But I figured you wouldn't want to come to the kitchen. Autumn is still mad at you."

He picked up the can, checked that the top was still on, and walked over to the painting on the far wall—the one of the forest and river. Cody went to the bathroom. When he returned to the big room, Mr. Bird was standing by the larger table, squeezing paint out of tubes onto a flat piece of wood. Mostly white paint, it looked like. While Cody ate breakfast, Mr. Bird set up a small stepladder and climbed it with the flat piece of wood in one hand and two paintbrushes in the other.

Cody was fascinated. Why was he painting over something that was already there? Why did he have two brushes? And why was the peanut butter smooth? Crunchy was better. With his mouth full, he asked a question at the same time that Mr. Bird said something.

"Why are you—"

"We have to—"

They both stopped.

"Sorry, Cody, what were you asking?"

He swallowed. "Well, I was wondering why you're painting over the top of the sky in that picture. It's already blue."

The man turned around on his ladder. "That's a great question," he said. "Short answer—it's not the right color blue. Longer answer has to do with painting in oils, but we don't have time for that now. Let's think about you and your parents."

He turned around and kept talking while he dabbed at the sky. "I want to be clear. Your dad never talked about being evicted? Even though it was going to happen soon?"

"No."

"Or where you would move?"

"No."

He used the smaller brush to paint over the wisps of sky between the leaves of one of the trees. "So you don't know where your dad is, and he doesn't know where you are." He sighed. "What about your mom?"

Cody didn't answer. Mr. Bird painted in silence for a moment, then tried again.

"Look, you ran away from home and ended up here. How long can you stay? What's your official address? We have to talk to someone from your past life. We can't find your dad. What about your mom? You said she used to care about you. And she's not dead. So where is she?"

Cody didn't like talking about his mom. It had been a while since he saw her. When did he and Dad take the bus out there—a month ago? More. There was snow on the ground. Mr. Bird went on painting.

Wait, how was he doing that?

"The sky is higher now. Is that what you're doing—making it higher?"

Mr. Bird turned around. "Higher?"

"It seems farther away from the ground now. The stream and rocks are lower. How did you do that?"

"I'm lightening the color in layers, so the eye travels up the painting and the sky seems to take up more space. But the way you put it is exactly right. The sky *is* higher now, isn't it?" He put his head on one side to stare at Cody. "You were interested in that painting in the hall too. You like art, hey?"

Cody nodded.

"Well, keep watching." He went back to putting dabs of lighter color into the sky. A minute later, in a casual voice, he asked, "Do you know where your mom is?"

Cody nodded.

"Good. Is she nearby? Can we talk to her?"

He nodded again.

Two hours later they were in the car, heading west out of the city. Cody didn't have an address or phone number for

Mom, but it only took a few minutes on the internet and three phone calls to find her and arrange a visit. Mr. Bird did it. While he was googling and phoning, and changing into a button-down shirt and khakis, Cody cleaned the brushes. Mr. Bird had showed him how. The flat piece of wood was called a palette. Where you mix your paints. Cody cleaned that too.

Now they were on the 401 West, heading for the Clarkson Center for Women, in a suburb outside Toronto. His mom was there serving a two-year sentence for theft under five thousand dollars.

They had an appointment for 10:45.

Beyond the highway guardrails, the city flashed by in concrete blocks and billboards.

"How are you feeling?" Mr. Bird asked.

Cody shrugged. This visit wasn't his decision. As they followed the voice of the GPS tracker—*take the next exit, turn left onto Spring Street, in one kilometer your destination will be on the right*—Cody wondered what his mom could do for him, and why Mr. Bird insisted on seeing her.

The detention center was the size of a small public school. The visitors room had a vinyl floor, small windows with bars on them, and tables with quiet people sitting and talking. Lots of women and babies and Kleenex. Not too many men, or smiles. Pretty much like the last time Cody was there. He and Mr. Bird found an empty table and sat down to wait.

A minute later, Mom came in with a guard, who stayed in the doorway with her arms crossed in front of her. Everyone looked up and away again. Mom walked slowly into the room, checking around in case of trouble. Cody knew that walk. He did it too. He stood up and gave a small wave.

He was trying to work out how he felt. Having a mom in prison usually felt weird, because no one else had one. Here and now, it wasn't weird to have a mom in prison. Everyone in this room was in prison. Even the guards were in prison. Cody didn't have to put Mom in a special place—sad, bad, unlucky, wrong. She was normal. Here, she was normal.

Mom smiled past Cody. He turned. Autumn's dad was on his feet, nodding. Mom pointed with a trembling finger. You'd swear she was seeing a vision.

"You!" She took a shuddering breath and staggered, barely keeping her balance. She was vibrating like an alarm clock. Other visitors looked over.

"Stouffer, you okay?" called a guard.

"I knew Cody would not come with his father," she said, talking right at Mr. Bird. "I knew he would come with a protector. And here you are. What is your name?"

"Hello, Mrs. Stouffer. My name is Tom Bird. And I want to ask—"

"Bird?" she interrupted. "Like that?" She pointed past them at the window behind, her eyes narrow like pinholes in a white sheet.

Cody turned to follow her finger. There was movement in the window frame. A black bird fluttered against the bars. The window was open to the spring day. The bird called into the visitors room.

"Save him!" Mom called out in a loud voice. "Save him, Bird."

She swayed, then fell to the floor in a dead faint. Other visitors pushed back chairs and stood up, looking concerned. The bird—a crow—gave a clear caw and flew off.

Cody was overwhelmed by a tidal wave of embarrassment. He wished he could disappear. Even here, Mom couldn't act like other moms.

That was the end of the visit. They rolled Mom out of the room on a stretcher. Mr. Bird gave one of the guards his cell phone number. He and Cody headed for the prison gates.

Mr. Bird drove back the same way they came. His face was set. He was thinking hard.

Cody cleared his throat. "About what Mom said about you as my, uh, protector. Did you believe her? How could she know stuff like that? She doesn't know you."

Mr. Bird changed lanes for the highway access. "Do you think she was lying? Why would she lie?"

"I don't know! But it's crazy."

Mr. Bird nodded. "That's right. You don't *know*."

They merged with highway traffic. The sun broke from the clouds and flashed on the chrome of all the cars. Cody squinted. It was suddenly hard to see. Traffic slowed down.

Mr. Bird's cell phone rang. He pushed a button on the car radio. Now the phone rang through that. He pushed another button and said hello.

"This is the Clarkson Center calling for Tom Bird."

"Speaking."

"We have an update on Rhonda Gail Stouffer. She is resting comfortably after her incident. And she has a message for . . . Bird."

"What is the message?"

"She says please and thank you."

Silence.

"Do you want me to repeat the message?"

"No, no, I get it. Thanks for passing it on."

Cody felt like he was listening to a regular radio broadcast, like his mom's message was part of the news and sports. Governments, hockey teams, please and thank you.

The rest of the drive was mostly silent. Driving over

the Bloor Viaduct, he asked a question he'd been dreading.

"What are you going to do?"

"I don't know."

"What's going to happen to me?"

He didn't get an answer until they were pulling into the drive.

"I have no idea, Cody. I'll talk to my wife and then . . . I don't know."

The garage was empty. The other car was gone. Mr. Bird explained that Autumn and her mom were at the community center. "Let's join them."

"Okay," said Cody.

"Give me five minutes and we'll walk together. It's not far."

Cody walked up and down the driveway until Mr. Bird came out in jeans and a sweatshirt. They set off together.

A few doors down, Cody heard a rustling behind some elaborate shrubbery and spied a familiar dark hair bun. A girl glided away across the lawn. It was Isabel from school. Invisible Isabel, who saw and heard everything. Where was she going? What was she doing here? What had she seen?

Not the strangest thing that had happened today. But another strange thing.

AUTUMN

"Here you go, Mr. Simpson." Autumn handed him a plate piled high with a turkey sandwich, celery and carrots, a chocolate chip cookie, and an apple. "I know you don't eat red meat, so I made you a turkey sandwich instead of roast beef."

"You are an angel." He winked at her as she slipped him an extra cookie. "You remind me so much of my daughter." He smiled.

"I know. You tell me that every time I see you."

"Well, you do! She was always kind like you. Always thinking of other people." He took a bite of his sandwich. "Mmm. That's good. No one makes a better turkey sandwich. She's going to come visit me, you know."

"For Christmas, right? You must be so excited to see her." Mr. Simpson nodded happily and took another bite as Autumn walked back toward the kitchen. He hadn't seen his daughter in years. His wife had taken her and left him when he went back to prison for the third or fourth time. But he had been out and clean for years, and Autumn had helped him find his daughter and reconnect. He had been telling anyone who would listen that they had made plans to get together this year over the holidays.

"You're so good with him." Autumn's mother was clearing a table near the kitchen door. "He's always telling me how much you—"

"Remind him of his daughter. I know." Autumn grinned. "I just have to do another walk around with the coffee and I'll get started on the dishes."

"I think Lucy beat you to it." Her mom nodded to another regular volunteer who was making the rounds and filling mugs. "I wanted to talk to you anyway. Can you grab that pile of dishes for me?"

Autumn picked up the plates and followed her mother into the kitchen, dumping them in the sink and running water over them. She squeezed a generous splash of dish soap and rolled up her sleeves.

"So? What did you want to talk about?"

"Cody."

Autumn rolled her eyes. "Do we have to? I'm so sick of talking about Cody. And seeing Cody. And dealing with Cody and his problems. I should never have helped him," she grumbled, sponging off a plate and clanking it into the drying rack.

"Rinse that," her mother ordered. "And you can't mean that, Autumn."

"I do mean that! Ever since I brought him home, everything has been about Cody!" She rinsed the plate and handed it to her mom to dry.

"I suspect nothing has been about Cody for most of his life."

"Maybe. But that doesn't make it okay to be racist."

"No," her mother agreed. "It doesn't. And it's okay to be upset about that. And to tell him he's wrong."

Autumn nodded and handed her mother another plate. "Okay. But when is he going home?"

"I don't know. I need to talk to your dad. I'm not sure he has much of a home."

"But why can't he stay with someone else? An aunt or an uncle or something. Why is it our responsibility to take care of him?"

"Autumn, you brought him into our lives. I have to believe you ran into him for a reason. He may not have anyone else." She put the plate down and turned to her daughter. "Do you remember the Grandfather Teachings? What does the wolf represent?"

"Humility," Autumn replied automatically. She had learned the Grandfather Teachings when she was small.

"Right. Humility. We're no better than anyone else. We have to remember that and not act selfishly."

Autumn nodded. "I'll try," she promised.

"You'll try what?" her dad asked. He and Cody stood in the doorway to the kitchen.

"Nothing," she mumbled, avoiding Cody's eyes.

"Why don't you show Cody around while I help your mom finish the dishes?"

She dried her hands on a towel and walked toward Cody.

"Come on," she muttered, leading the way back into the main room, where people were chatting noisily, finishing their lunches, playing cards and laughing together. A typical Saturday at the community center. "Probably not your kind of place," she told him loudly. "Lots of Indians here."

As she watched his face turn crimson and thought of her mother's words, she suddenly wished she could take her comment back.

CODY

Cody followed Autumn through the crowded room. Two rows of cafeteria tables with an aisle up the middle, armchairs and sofas along the wall, and not an empty seat. He couldn't help noticing how popular she was. Everyone knew her. They looked up from their trays of food. They smiled, nodded, waved. Old and young, single men or families with little kids, in wheelchairs or walkers, they all had a smile for Autumn. Cody, walking behind her, was ignored. Which made a kind of sense. She was special here, and he was not. She stood out here, and he did not.

Funny that she would say this was not his kind of place. He felt fine here—way more comfortable than he did, say, at school during lunch. No one in this community center was looking down on him, the way a lot of them did at school. The only one here who was sneering was Autumn. The way she said that bit about there being lots of Indians.

People here were happy to get a free meal. Happy to hang out with other people as poor as they were. It was a kind of safety. Belonging. Something Cody was not used to feeling at school.

Maybe everyone ignoring him meant that he belonged here?

He followed Autumn back to the kitchen, a cube of a room, as tall as it was wide. Concrete blocks, white paint, a long metal counter. Lots of busy people tidying up. Cody ducked out of the way of a woman with a tray full of dirty dishes. She carried it to a sink and slid the whole thing into a dishwasher. Dr. Bird was pointing at someone, asking them to do... something. She gave Cody a quick reserved smile, then went back to work.

What was she thinking—that it was time to kick him out of her house, or hand him over to the authorities? Did she know about Mom's message? Had Mr. Bird told her?

Meanwhile, there was this big round plate of sandwiches on brown bread, cut in half. Some kind of meat with lettuce and tomato. Cody had never eaten a sandwich like that in his life. But it had been a while since breakfast. Quite a while.

Beside the tray of sandwiches was a plate of carrot sticks, a basket of apples, and a big tray of cookies. It all looked pretty good.

He heard Autumn's voice. "Cody, do you want to take one of those sandwiches—"

"Yes," he said, reaching.

"—and offer it to a guest? Lunch is almost over, but I think there are some new arrivals, and they'll be hungry."

It took him a second to work it out. She wasn't offering him lunch. She was telling him to carry lunch to someone else.

"Oh. Right. Sure," he said.

"Here, let me show you how." She pulled on a pair of sterile gloves from a box on the counter and made up a plate for him.

"Look around the dining room for someone who hasn't gotten anything to eat. Okay? Take the tray—carefully."

"Sure."

"And tell everyone we're closing down soon. They only have a few more minutes to get a meal."

Autumn moved quickly, surely. She'd done this before. Cody had to keep glancing down to make sure the tray was level.

He walked down the aisle between the two rows of tables, checking both sides of the dining room for someone to give the tray to. He didn't see anyone who looked as hungry as he felt.

Cody came to a table of four old ladies playing cards. The one shuffling had gray hair and a tan face and long fingers with rings on most of them. Straight bony nose and a big jaw. Come to think of it, she looked like a—what was the word Autumn used—Indigenous. She looked Indigenous. Were there lots of other Indigenous folks around, like Autumn said? Cody couldn't tell.

This lady brought the two halves of the deck together and riffled them to make a waterfall shuffle. Pretty cool. Cody stood quietly next to the table until she noticed him.

"Uhhh, they'll be closing the kitchen soon," he said. "So I was wondering if you . . . if I could . . ."

"Do you want to join us?" said the shuffler. "Is that what you're saying? You sure look hungry. Move over, Cheryl, let the boy sit down. He looks like he hasn't eaten in a week."

"No," said Cody. "That's not—"

"Please. We insist, don't we, girls?"

The other ladies smiled. Cheryl, who had prune wrinkles and hair the color of a school bus, shoved herself to one side, pulled up an empty chair, and patted it.

"Sit here, honey," she said. "Tuck in."

Cody tried to tell them he wasn't here for a free meal—that he was helping out. It didn't help when a regular helper—a woman with clean hair and an apron, carrying a metal coffeepot—came over to say hi to Cody and welcome him to the community center.

"You're among friends here," she said, with a big white smile. "We'll always be happy to see you. Won't we, Cheryl?"

She refilled Cheryl's mug while Cheryl nodded her yellow head enthusiastically. "Thanks, Lucy," she said.

Cody didn't know what to do. He was hungry. And the tray was right there. And everyone was smiling at him, expecting him to sit down and dig in.

The shuffling lady dealt out the whole deck, four neat stacks of cards. "Do you play bridge?" she said to Cody. "If you want to learn, you can look on with Cheryl. She's a great teacher."

He wavered. He was hungry, all right. But he couldn't sit down now, could he? What would Autumn say? And here she came. She was talking with an older guy who looked kind of tough. Broad shoulders, big hands.

"My daughter used to say that too," he told her.

They stopped at Cody's table. "What are you doing?" Autumn asked him. "You know you can't sit there, right?"

Everyone talked at once.

"I thought he was a guest," said Lucy the coffee pourer.

"No, he's supposed to be helping."

"Let the boy eat," said the shuffler and dealer.

"I—I—" Cody shrugged helplessly and spilled some of the juice.

"Jeez, Cody," said Autumn.

Now the tough guy stepped forward. "Why aren't you helping this young woman?" he said. "She's an angel. And what are you? A punk."

"You don't understand, Mr. Simpson," said Autumn. "Cody is—"

"A punk," said Mr. Simpson. "I know his kind. He doesn't belong here."

"I was *trying*—" Cody's voice shot into falsetto when he noticed Mr. Simpson's hands. They were clenched into fists.

"Don't be silly," said the dealer, frowning at her cards. "Of course he belongs here. Look at him."

"If he belongs here, he should do what he's told."

"And *you* should leave him alone. He's hungry. Let him eat. I bid one heart."

"Pass," said Cheryl.

The old guy glared.

Cody felt like a dead leaf in a windstorm, blown here and there by more powerful forces, helpless and fragile and unattached.

AUTUMN

Watching Cody surrounded by Cheryl and her gang, and Lucy, and being . . . embraced by them made Autumn's stomach feel weird. Kinda sick and droopy. Like going up the hill of a roller coaster slowly—knowing you're going to reach the top and there's no way of stopping it. And then you hang there at the top. Staring down at a drop you know is probably going to kill you or make you throw up or, at the very least, make you scream until it feels like your lungs will explode.

Watching Cody being befriended by the group—*her* group—felt like that. And there he was, trying to take one of their sandwiches like he hadn't eaten in days when she knew for a fact he had eaten breakfast that morning.

Autumn was glaring her death stare at Cody when she caught her mom moving toward her out of the corner of her eye.

She took a deep breath. She could hear her mom in her head before she got within a couple of meters of her.

Try to be kind to him, Autumn, her mother said inside her head. *He hasn't been as lucky as you have.*

"All right," Autumn said out loud.

"What?" Cody was looking at her, like he didn't know what to do next.

"Nothing. Why don't you go ahead and eat and then you can help tidy up after."

If she had smacked him in the head with a giant fish, Cody couldn't possibly have looked any more surprised than he did right then. Because he didn't expect her to be nice. He didn't expect *anyone* to be nice to him. And for the first time, Autumn could see how much that sucked. She didn't like Cody. But she realized her mom was right. Cody had nothing and no one who cared about him. And maybe—just maybe—he deserved just a little bit of kindness. Or at least not blatant hostility.

"Ummm. Okay. Thanks."

"Sure. And careful playing cards with this bunch. They're ruthless." She winked at Cheryl and put a hand on Mr. Simpson's arm. "It's okay, Mr. Simpson. Cody is staying with us for a while. Why don't you show me those pictures of your daughter again?"

Autumn passed her mother, who nodded her approval. Autumn felt her chest swell with pride.

She could be nice, she realized. She didn't have to stoop to his level.

She was scraping the last of the dishes into the garbage and loading them into a dish rack, ready to go into the dishwasher, when Cody appeared in the doorway, nibbling the last of the fruit from around the core of an apple. He tossed it toward the garbage.

"Hey!" The core had bounced off Autumn's stomach before dropping to the floor. "What the hell?"

"Oh no! Sorry!" Cody rushed forward and grabbed it off the floor, dropping it into the garbage before wiping at her shirt with a filthy towel he got from the pile of dirty laundry.

"Stop! You're making it worse! Jeez. What is wrong with you?"

"Nothing! It was an accident! Why are you such a . . ."

"Such a what?" Autumn asked, her eyes narrowing, daring him to answer.

"Nothing." Cody dropped the dirty dish towel back into the bin of laundry.

"No. Go ahead. What did you want to call me?"

"Nothing! Just forget it, okay?"

"Forget what?" Autumn's mother asked, bringing in the last of the dishes from the tables.

"Nothing," Autumn muttered, glaring at Cody.

"Yeah, nothing," he agreed.

"Okay. Cody, can you wipe down the tables for me?"

"All of them?" he asked.

Autumn rolled her eyes. "Yes. We need all of them wiped

down. There's a spray bottle right over there and some clean rags under that cabinet."

"Okay." Cody took the supplies and headed into the dining room.

Autumn took a deep breath as her mother turned toward her.

"I'm trying! I swear. But he's just so . . . I mean, he can't even . . . He called me . . . ARRGH!" Autumn threw the dishrag down and stalked out of the kitchen, grabbing her jacket on her way.

"I'm going to walk home on my own," Autumn said as she pushed through the double doors into a rainstorm that immediately soaked her to the skin.

Just as she arrived on Bloor Street, she saw them.

"Autumn?" Connor and his buddies were standing in the bus shelter, looking dry and warm.

Perfect. Just perfect.

CODY

Cody was used to wiping down surfaces. For years he had kept the kitchen table and counters clean to discourage roaches. Wiping the community center tables now, rinsing the cloth and wiping some more, brought back all sorts of grim memories. His cheek ached from his dad's shoe. Was that only a couple of days ago? It seemed like a year.

One more table to go.

"Bye, Cody!" said Cheryl with the yellow hair on her way out.

"See you next time, darlin'!" called the Indigenous-looking lady, waving at him with her long, card-shuffling fingers. She was wearing bright red stretch pants—the same kind as a woman who lived in Cody's old building. In a real sense, he belonged in this community center more than he did in Autumn's house.

He had a quick thought. Should he go after Cheryl or the card shuffler? They must live nearby. They were friendly. Would they take him in? They would see him for who he really was—one of their own.

What was he doing hanging around a mansion in Rosedale? He belonged here in St. James Town.

Still, only a few minutes later he was on his way back to the mansion. He was sitting in the back seat of Dr. Bird's car. It was smaller than her husband's, but the seats were just as soft. Mr. Bird was in the front. He turned around to ask Cody if he knew Autumn's plans for the afternoon.

"She didn't say anything to me."

Dr. Bird drove faster than her husband. She took a left turn at Parliament Street on the yellow light, accelerated past the graveyard, and took the right turn onto Bloor on another yellow. Cody hung on to the armrest. They got to the Bird garage before he could catch his breath.

There was a message from Autumn on Dr. Bird's phone.

"*Back later.* What does that mean?" she asked her husband.

There was tension in the air. Cody sat still. He didn't even undo his seat belt.

"Don't worry. I'm sure she's okay."

They took a moment to squeeze hands before getting out of the car. Cody felt awkward but also strangely warm. They were *worried* about their daughter. That was a nice thing. He didn't know what it was like to have someone worry about him.

A couple of years ago, he and Watch Out Dennis from down the hall stayed out all night. Dennis and his mom lived in Montreal now, but before they moved, he and Cody used to get into trouble for breaking windows and setting trash fires. One night, climbing onto a roof of a construction site in Cabbagetown, Dennis had knocked over the ladder and shouted "Watch out!" into the darkness. No one was around to hear. They'd stayed up there until the workers came in the morning. When Cody showed up for breakfast, his dad had said, "Oh, there you are." And yawned.

Mr. and Dr. Bird worrying about Autumn—even though she had a cell phone in her pocket and even though she was nowhere near dumb enough to climb a rickety ladder with a crazy friend—was kind of nice.

When they all got out of the car, Cody wondered what to do. Should he go with them into the house? Should he cross the yard and let himself into the studio? Or should he wait for them to tell him what to do?

He waited. They asked what he wanted to do. Which was not a question he got asked very often. He shrugged.

"I'll be in the studio painting, if you don't mind," said Mr. Bird.

"Can I watch?"

"If you want to."

Cody nodded vigorously.

"Okay, I'll see you there after I put on a painting shirt." He headed off.

Dr. Bird and Cody were alone in the garage. She put her hand on his arm. "I heard about what happened at the prison. Your mother cares about you, doesn't she?"

"I guess so." Mind you, if she really cared, maybe she wouldn't have stolen all that stuff in the first place. And gotten caught and sent to jail.

"She can't act for you, but she has faith, and she has her voice. She's asked for help."

Dr. Bird's face was open, empty, clean, like a fresh sheet of paper. She stood next to Cody, but she was looking at him from a long way off. It was kind of intimidating. He knew that Mr. Bird was truly upset and puzzled about him. But he had no idea what Dr. Bird thought.

A couple of hours later, Mr. Bird was in a high state of paint. It was on his hands and arms, his sleeves and pants. He climbed down the ladder and stepped away from the forest scene he was still working on.

"What do you think, Cody? The tree trunks came out well, eh?"

Cody looked up from his piece of paper. He'd been sketching Mr. Bird as he painted.

"The picture is sharper now. It's like"—his hand made a twirling gesture—"like when you twist the focus knob and everything gets clearer."

Mr. Bird looked pleased. He put his palette in the sink and pushed his hair off his face. Now his hair had paint in it.

"But why didn't you paint it that way the first time?" Cody asked. "If you wanted the tree trunks darker, why not paint them darker?"

Mr. Bird nodded. "Brown is not a primary color," he said. "A bunch of colors go together to make it. You mix red and yellow to get orange, then add blue to darken it to brown. How dark the brown is depends on how much blue you put in. The great thing about painting in oils is that you can layer the colors on top of each other. If you want to darken the tree trunks, put a layer of blue on top of the lighter brown. Which is what I just did. Do you understand?"

"Sort of."

There's blue in brown? Cody peered closely at the tree trunks in the picture. You don't get it right the first time. You keep on adding layers to make the color better. That sounded like a life lesson.

"Only *sort of*. And are you only *sort of* interested?"

"No!" Cody pushed the drawing paper away. He didn't like his sketches anyway. "No. I'm real interested."

"Good." Mr. Bird looked pleased again. "We'll talk about colors some more later. I should probably go inside and take a shower now."

While he wiped his hands, Cody collected the paints and brushes.

On his way out of the studio, Mr. Bird glanced at the sketches.

"Not bad," he said. "But you want to relax. Don't be afraid of mistakes. You're drawing too much from the shoulder. Next time, try to loosen your elbow and wrist."

"What do you mean?" Too much shoulder? How could you have too much shoulder? Or not enough shoulder?

"I'll show you next time. Dinner in a half hour. You can eat pad Thai, right? Autumn loves my pad Thai. Come over to the house any time."

And he was gone.

Cody got busy with the paintbrushes and turpentine. His cleaning motions seemed stiff. Was he using too much shoulder?

Dinner was awkward. Three of them in the kitchen. Autumn wanted to eat in her room. Mr. Bird served Cody first. He started right in, but Dr. Bird put her hand on his arm and told him to wait. That was embarrassing. Chewing and swallowing spicy noodles, pretending he wasn't coughing, pretending nothing was happening.

When they were all served, Dr. Bird closed her eyes and said something Cody didn't understand. When she was done, they sat silently, then started eating. Mr. Bird got up and put on some music. Nothing Cody had ever heard before. He ate quickly, afraid to lift his eyes from the food in case they were staring. He wished Autumn was around. Even if she was mad at him, she was someone he could talk to.

He finished first, carried his empty plate to the sink, and rinsed it off, like he did at home. He did this without thinking. But where was the soap and towel? He turned with the plate in his hand.

"Oh, thanks, Cody. Just put that in the dishwasher," said Mr. Bird. He murmured something to his wife. She murmured something back.

Cody checked around the kitchen. He'd seen commercials for dishwashing soap. He'd seen happy women holding up clean glasses. But what did dishwashers look like on the outside?

Cody panicked. Was this built-in thing with dials and numbers a dishwasher? Nope. No shelves. How about this square thing with a handle and a thermometer? Nope. It was too small and it smelled like pizza. That thing over there couldn't be a dishwasher—it had to be an oven. He checked to make sure. Yup, an oven.

His heart pounded. The world was weaving and waving around him.

"Sorry," he blurted, dropping plate and cutlery on the counter with a clatter, "but I can't find the dishwasher. I'm sorry. I'm tired. I should go to bed. Thanks for dinner. Sorry. And for the sweatshirt and the other stuff. The bed—thanks for that too. And the drawing lesson. Sorry about my wrist and shoulder. I know I should be better at . . . everything. I have to go."

He raced out of the kitchen into—oh no!—a closet with shelves of food going all the way up to the ceiling. Wrong door! He stumbled back to the kitchen and followed Mr. Bird's pointing hand.

"Sorry," he said. "I'm okay. Really."

The hall. The back door. The yard. The familiar studio.

After a dozen deep breaths, he poured himself a glass of water and thought about what was going on with him and Autumn's family.

He was scared of them. He was scared all through dinner. That scene with the empty plate was about more than a dishwasher.

But he wasn't scared when Autumn first told him her background. At first he was relieved, because he didn't have to worry about measuring up to her. The pressure was off. It didn't matter about Autumn's house and all. He had something they did not have. They could never catch up to him.

So why was he scared now? They were still Indigenous.

What had happened? What changed?

Hard to say.

Cody was ready to trust the Birds now. At the end of his dream, he knew his only chance was to leap into the ditch hoping that Autumn and her dad would catch him. It was hard to look down on people you trusted. Mom's message to Mr. Bird showed that she trusted him too. But what if the Birds didn't do what Mom asked? What if they didn't save Cody? Maybe that was why he was scared now. Hope was scary. Especially if you were not sure you were worth saving.

Cody put on Mr. Bird's sweatpants and rinsed his face. He sat on the couch, staring up at the painting with its fresh layer of color. The darker tree trunks were sharper, clearer, and somehow closer than they were. He must remember to ask Mr. Bird if drawing something darker moved it to the front of the picture.

The peacefulness of the scene spread outward. Cody felt it in his arms and legs, in his stomach, in his head. He relaxed.

It had been a big day. And it wasn't over yet. The studio door opened and a stranger blundered in.

"I saw the light and knew you'd be here."

When she raised her head, he saw that she was not a stranger at all. In fact, she was the most likely person to show up. Her face was twisted into something between a frown and a sneeze. Was she still mad at him?

"Listen. This is important," she said, taking a step forward.

Cody was on his feet. "What is?"

"What I'm telling you. Why won't you listen?"

She waved her arms around. Cody couldn't help thinking that her shoulder didn't seem tight at all. Maybe he should wave before sketching.

"Are you okay, Autumn?" he asked.

AUTUMN

Was she okay? Was he serious? Did she look like she was okay? She was about as far from okay as you could possibly get. But the number of people she could talk to right now who weren't friends of either Connor or Mia was exactly zero.

Well . . . it was one. And he was standing right in front of her.

Autumn plunked herself down on the sofa and pulled a pillow into her lap.

"Everything is such a mess," she told him. God, what was she doing? Was she really *that* desperate for friends?

Yes. She kind of was.

She had tried to text a couple of her old friends from the track team. When she had been on the track team. Before she started hanging out with Mia, who thought breaking a sweat was disgusting. She probably would have stayed on the team even with Mia's disapproval—she loved running more than anything—but there was that one time when they were all goofing around in Connor's backyard, listening to him brag about how fast he was and how he could beat anyone there. When he took off running, Autumn went with him. And then flew past him. And then left him behind. She turned around, expecting everyone to laugh or clap or congratulate her. But no one said a word. And Connor was mortified. He stuttered out something about letting her win, and she hated to admit it . . . but she went along with it.

She quit the track team the next day.

And she missed it like crazy. Suddenly she was sitting with the popular kids and going to parties with them on the weekends instead of training or staying in and watching movies with the girls from the team. She left them behind. She traded in her shorts and sweats for high-rise jeans and heels and makeup and sitting next to Connor and listening to him talk about how great he was at sports while she sat quietly, bored out of her mind, watching her old running friends laugh uproariously at something that she just knew she'd like way more than anything her new friends had to say.

She had texted a couple of them to see if they wanted to hang out and waited nervously, hands sweating, but only one responded to remind her that she had ditched them for the popular kids.

So she catches Mia and Connor wrapped around each other, and her old friends won't talk to her because she ditched them for Mia and Connor, and she walks home from the community center and sees, of all people, CONNOR?

Yeah. She wasn't doing great. Thanks for asking, though, Cody.

It got worse after that. Because Connor wanted to talk about it and explain to her that *nothing* had happened. That the kiss she saw was literally *nothing* and that Mia meant nothing to him and *she* was kissing him and he was about to push her away when Autumn walked in . . . And things could just go back to normal if she let it.

And she was tempted. She hated to admit it, but having things go back to the way they were just a few days ago when she was sitting in the cafeteria gossiping with Mia and Aliyah while Connor draped an arm over her shoulder that she couldn't decide if she actually liked or not but tolerated because it made her feel important? She was ashamed to admit she considered it for about half a second. Until she saw Mia come out of the corner store and hand an energy drink to Connor.

"Oh, hey," she said to Autumn. Just like that. "Oh, hey." And Autumn knew that no matter what Connor was saying, there was something between him and Mia and there was no way she could go back to the way things were.

So she left.

Just turned and walked away from the guy she had called her boyfriend, even though she didn't really like him very much, and the girl she had called her best friend, even though they had absolutely nothing in common.

Now she had no one except this scrawny kid in front of her who had infiltrated her home and squirmed his way into her family.

"No," Autumn responded. "I'm not okay. Everything is such a mess! I don't have any friends. I have no one to talk to. My friends—my REAL friends—are mad at me for ditching them and I can't even blame them. And my new friends . . . well, they're not really friends at all and I guess I knew that all along and what kind of person ditches their friends anyway?" she finished breathlessly while Cody studied her from behind his too-long hair. "I suck," she told him.

"No, you don't," he said.

"I do. I really do." Autumn took a breath. She was sick and tired of keeping all the things she really wanted to say to people bottled up. "And you know what, Cody? You kind of suck too."

"I—" That was all. He looked like he was going to argue but then he just . . . stopped. He closed his eyes and took a long, slow, shuddering breath and then breathed it out slowly. Autumn thought he actually looked like he was thinking about what she had said. Turning it over in his head. She wondered what he saw there. Did he even know how hurtful he had been? How narrow-minded and mean?

She knew he probably learned this stuff from his dad, who was obviously pretty horrible. If he beat up his own kid,

Autumn could totally see him being a racist too. Cody had to learn it somewhere. But that did not excuse what he'd said. Everyone had to learn to think for themselves. She did. She knew her parents probably weren't right about everything. They wanted her to think for herself! But she suspected Cody never learned that lesson.

He looked like he was going to cry.

"Do you want me to leave?" he said.

"Huh? No! I want you to listen. Some of the things you said to me and my parents . . . It's not okay to talk to people like that! And I should have said something sooner, but using slurs is . . . It's gross. It makes me feel gross. You called us Indians. You said my uncle wore a costume. You looked down on the people at the center. None of that is okay, Cody! It's racist!"

Autumn was breathing hard, and she could feel her nails digging into the palms of her hands. But she felt better. She had wanted to say something to him for so long. She looked at Cody, whose eyes were open now, staring at her. His face was red.

"I didn't know," he said.

"What part didn't you know?"

"Any of it. I didn't think it was racist—just kind of funny because it was . . . different . . . I guess."

"We're all different. I mean, I think having a dad who beats you up is different. But I don't think it's funny."

Cody dropped his eyes. He was ashamed. Autumn almost felt sorry she'd said that about his dad. He looked straight down when he spoke, aiming his words at the floor. Straight down, not off to the side. Autumn had read a book that said when people were lying they often looked to the side. Maybe Cody wasn't lying.

"I didn't know it was racist to think about you that way because I didn't know anything about Indigenous people. I didn't know you. I guess that's how racism works. But I know you now."

He looked up. His eyes were shining.

"And I know this. Autumn, you literally picked me up off the street and brought me home with you. Anyone who does that for a total stranger does *not* suck."

It was the nicest thing he had ever said to her, and Autumn had an overwhelming desire to hug him. Or cry.

She did neither. She just awkwardly nodded at him.

"I don't have anywhere to sit at lunch now," she blurted out. God! Why was she suddenly telling this kid her life story?

He shrugged.

"You can sit with me if you want." His face burned suddenly. "I mean . . . I know it's not the same and we're not really friends or whatever . . . but if you want . . . you don't have to, though . . ." He trailed off.

She smiled suddenly. The first time she had ever smiled at him, she realized.

"Thanks, Cody," she said, and left him there among her dad's paints and brushes and turpentine and canvases.

Somehow, she thought, he looked like he belonged there.

CODY

Sunday was one of the nicest days Cody could remember. Considering that he had no home, no family nearby, no money or job, and no idea of his future, he should have been too scared to breathe. But he wasn't. He woke up on the couch with a smile on his face.

He was happy because of Autumn. He knew her better now. Last night, staggering into the studio, she was not the cool, popular girl he was used to seeing at school. She was scared and mad, and she thought she was awful. She was just like him. That was surprising. And him being able to make her feel better about herself—that was even more surprising. Helping someone feel better made *you* feel good too. He didn't like her calling him a racist. That was hard to hear. It was probably hard for her to say too. Autumn was always nice to people. He owed her an apology. That thought brought the smile back to his face. The apology would make him feel better too.

She was not mad at him anymore.

Friendship was better than anger. It was better than most

things. Cody had never had a friend like Autumn. Watch Out Dennis was fun, but you couldn't trust him. He'd let you down. One time, walking down Parliament Street late at night, a stranger grabbed Cody's arm. Dennis turned and ran before the stranger could say a word. Turned out he had thought Cody was someone else and let go of his arm. But Dennis was a block away by then.

Autumn would not have run away. No matter what the stranger did, she would not run away. She might have knocked him down. She might have fed him. But she would not have deserted Cody.

Friendship was a good reason to smile. Cody got up and dressed and headed over to the big house, and when he got to the kitchen, Mr. Bird was at the stove, shaking a frying pan. Dr. Bird was sitting at the table with a cup of coffee, and when she saw Cody she smiled and said, "Hi there!" He almost burst into tears. That's how happy he was.

The rest of the day lived up to the great start. First, he and Dr. Bird went to a store on the Danforth and bought clothes. Lots of them. Another pair of jeans, two shirts, underpants, two pairs of socks, and a black hoodie with red writing: WE THE NORTH. And no one had worn any of these before! Cody was the first one. He carried the clothes out of the store in a bag big enough for Santa.

Then, while the clothes were in the washing machine (Dr. Bird said you shouldn't wear clothes straight from the store), Cody went back to the studio to work on his drawing. He'd watched a bird through the window yesterday, fascinated by the way its wings and legs moved. He was drawing it, over and over, flying, landing in the grass, taking off. Cody was trying to keep his arm relaxed as he drew.

Autumn's dad came in to work on his forest painting and watched for a few minutes.

"I like that one," he said. He pointed at the lousiest of the sketches, one where the bird was hopping along, flapping its wings. The lines were all over the place.

"It's not very accurate," Cody said.

"No, but it's good. You drew it the right way. Relaxing, blanking your mind, letting your hand move over the page, you got a sense of what that crow feels. It's getting ready to fly and it's excited. Good for you."

Mr. Bird went to the worktable and started loading his palette.

Cody beamed happily.

Later that afternoon, he sat in a room at the front of the house, trying to draw Boomer, who was flopped on the couch beside him. He tried to empty his mind and let his arm go loose. The dog grumbled in his sleep and yawned wide enough to hold a melon. Autumn came in, sweat-shining and healthy, in shorts and a T-shirt.

"I thought I heard something. What are you doing here, Cody? No one ever comes here."

"Why not?" The room had two couches and a fireplace and a rug with a weird pattern, and a big window and a bookcase and a picture of three triangles on an orange background that looked like it was moving. And it smelled like summer. It was better than any room Cody had ever lived in.

"I don't know actually, but no one does."

He couldn't get his head around the idea of a place that was too big for you, a place with rooms you could ignore. If he lived here, he'd sit in every room every day, just to show the house he appreciated it.

Autumn went upstairs for a shower. When she came back down, they played a card game. It was her idea—he didn't know any games. In this one, the cards had pictures of food on them. What made it more confusing was that the food was stuff Cody didn't know and had never eaten. The idea was to collect sets of cards with the same kind of food. Cody didn't mind playing. He did not mind losing badly.

"Sorry I'm no good at this," he said, holding up a card that said—seriously—*SQUID NIGIRI 3*. Whatever that could possibly mean.

Dr. Bird came in with something in her hand.

"I found this in a drawer and thought maybe you could use it, Cody," she said. "In case you want to get in touch with anyone in the next little while. Here."

She handed him a cell phone. It was gray.

Wow. His own phone.

Autumn started to laugh, then stopped. What was wrong? She was blushing.

"I'm not laughing at you, Cody," she said. "It's an old phone, that's all." But her face remained flushed, darker than usual.

Later, she showed him how his phone worked. He didn't care that it was old. It was his—for now. Sitting on the couch beside the dog, she sent him a text from her phone. His first one.

Hi

He sent one back.

Who is this?

Autumn laughed and punched Cody on the arm. Boomer farted loudly. They got up together. They were both laughing. Cody grabbed his sketch and went back to the studio.

The air was warm. The leaves rustled in the gentle breeze.

That church up Glen Road rang its bell a few times. Yes, it was a good day. One of the best Cody could remember. The next day—Monday—started off okay. New clothes, new phone, walking to school with Autumn under cloudy skies. She seemed pretty tense. Like she was expecting something. Sure enough, trouble started the moment they got to the schoolyard.

AUTUMN

Connor and Mia were huddled together by the front entrance of the school, surrounded by all the popular kids. Aliyah was trying to shove her way in beside Mia, but someone new had taken her place.

Isabel.

Isabel who was invisible.

Isabel who saw everything but talked to no one.

Isabel who had never come within twenty feet of Mia was now standing right beside her, whispering to her and Connor. And looking right at Autumn and Cody.

"Oh crap," Autumn muttered.

"What?" Cody was as oblivious as always.

"Hey!" Mia called out across the lawn. "If it isn't the lovebirds."

"Oooohhhhhhh!" Aliyah purred at them. "It's the lovebirds!"

Autumn rolled her eyes. Aliyah never was very original. She felt Cody tense beside her and elbowed him.

"Don't," she whispered under her breath.

"Izzy has been telling us some very interesting things about you two." Mia smirked, throwing an arm around Isabel.

Izzy?

"Some *really* interesting things," Aliyah parroted.

"Oh yeah?" Autumn countered.

"Yeah." Mia nodded. "I hear you've been cheating on Connor with him." Her nose wrinkled as she lifted her chin toward Cody.

Autumn laughed. "So that's the story you're going with? You two snuck around behind *my* back!"

"Only after you started cheating with him! Izzy told us everything!"

Autumn shook her head and took a deep breath. She was not going to let them twist things around.

"*Izzy* doesn't know what she's talking about. And his name is Cody, by the way. He's in our social studies class, remember? He's staying with my family for a while. That's it. And you know it."

"All I know is that you better find somewhere else to sit for lunch." Mia tossed her hair and snuggled up against Connor. She grabbed Isabel's hand. "Your seat is taken."

"You couldn't pay me to sit with you," Autumn told her. "And I'd rather sit alone than listen to you talk about yourself," she shot at Connor.

She pushed past them and walked into the school, trying to ignore the sounds of the popular kids laughing at her.

Just like that, Autumn had been replaced.

CODY

Isabel's face was not its usual blank. She was exultant, fiercely joyful. She and Mia made an odd pair. Mia slinked along in a stringy way. Isabel clunked along after her like a bale of hay bouncing down the stairs.

Cody had seen Isabel's expression on someone else's face, but where? He followed Autumn all the way to her locker.

"Nowhere to go. No one to go there with. I've got no one," she said. "I've been canceled. Did you see that?"

"But didn't you say Mia wasn't a real friend and that you didn't like her? Now it's clear she doesn't like you either. So that's okay, right?"

She sighed. "You don't get it, Cody. I've got no one. If you don't have friends, who are you? If you don't belong to a group, who are you? I've got no one, so I am no one."

School hadn't started yet. The hall was empty. Autumn's voice echoed around. *I am no one.* Kind of spooky.

Cody didn't understand. Being upset that your friends didn't like you didn't make sense. If they didn't like you, then they weren't your friends. Right? Maybe friends mattered more if you were used to being cool together. Cody had never been cool. Never had many friends. He was amazed that Autumn—who had so much—was worried about Mia.

The bell rang, and the hall began to fill with shouting and shoving. Mia and Isabel and what's-her-name walked past without turning their heads. Mia was talking. Isabel and what's-her-name were nodding enthusiastically.

"Looks like she's just won the lottery," muttered Autumn.

That was where he'd seen that crazy joyful expression before. An old lady on the news with a winning ticket in her hand. Mia was Isabel's winning ticket. No wonder she was hanging on to her.

"Who is that with them?" he asked in a low voice. "I don't know her name."

"Huh?"

"The other girl. Not Isabel." Cody peered down the hall. "Oh well. She's gone now."

His locker was around the corner. "See you in social studies," he said. It was the only class they had together.

"But we'll sit together at lunch, right?" For a second she looked almost panicky. Did she really think he wouldn't sit with her?

He had the meal her dad gave him in his backpack. "Of course we'll eat together."

"Good."

And they did sit together. Mr. Bird's sandwiches were amazing. Rolled into a tube, leaking creamy gravy, they tasted somewhere between KFC and heaven. Licking his fingers, Cody noticed Autumn staring across the cafeteria at three girls drinking milkshakes that must have tasted awful, since they were making faces as they went down. Their short sleeves showed their muscles. They looked healthy enough to chew their table and spit it across the room. One of them was in Cody's English class. She spoke with an accent.

"I want to go running," said Autumn, still staring at them.

"How can you run when you're full of your dad's sandwiches?"

"I'm not full. I can't eat any more. Here, you finish mine."

"Done." Cody watched her head out the door of the cafeteria. She passed the table of cool kids without turning her head.

He checked out everyone at the table. Connor, Mia, Aliyah, and what's-her-name, with the black hair and glasses, who was always talking about the private school she was going to next year. What was her name anyway?

Isabel wasn't even at the table. What was Mia talking about?

No, wait—there she was! Cody had to smile. Even though she was at the cool kids' table, sitting right next to Mia, she was hard to notice.

Three periods later, Cody slipped into social studies class. The teacher had an announcement.

AUTUMN

It felt good to run. So good that Autumn nearly forgot all the drama for a minute.

Almost.

She couldn't forget, but she could push it away for a little while. So she pushed. And she ran.

It was harder than it used to be. She could feel her legs burning and her lungs struggling a little to keep up. But she'd run through it and her body would remember what it was like to fly.

She slowed down and walked a bit, her hands on her hips as she drew in deep gulps of air.

"Not bad," a voice called out from the sidelines, where a girl was stretching with her legs straight out in front of her.

"Thanks," she called back. Mira. One of the girls on the cross-country team. They had never been close, but they had been rivals on the team.

"You need to work on your breathing," Mira told her, standing up and pulling one leg up behind her.

"I know. I haven't run in a while."

Mira nodded but didn't say anything.

"I thought maybe I'd try out for the team again," Autumn said. She looked down, scraping the toe of her running shoe through the dirt. "I miss running a lot. And I miss the team." She felt her eyes prickle and willed herself not to cry.

Mira nodded again. "Well, see ya," she said before jogging toward the track.

Autumn felt her chest tighten. She tried not to care that every one of her teammates had written her off, because she couldn't blame them. She probably would have done the same. But she wished she could change it. Go back and ignore Mia and Aliyah and Connor and the rest of them, and just keep running.

"Hey!" Mira was standing on the track.

"Yeah?"

"A couple of us come early to warm up and train before practice. You can come sometime if you want."

"Really? Yeah! I mean . . . absolutely. I'd love to. Thanks!" Autumn gushed.

"Cool. We're here by seven."

"Cool! I'll be there. Here. I'll be here!" She waved. Oh my God. Could she be any less cool? She didn't even care. She was going to run again!

Autumn threw herself down on the ground with more

enthusiasm than she thought was humanly possible and started stretching.

If she was going to try out for the team again, she needed to get back into shape. She bent one leg behind her and bent over her other leg as far as she could go, grinning widely the entire time.

CODY

Social studies was last period. With five minutes to go, Ms. Koon announced a project on "something that makes society better." That's what she said.

"It could be a paper on recycling, for instance. But the project doesn't have to be written down. It could be a poster, or an interview, or a video. Just something that makes society a better place. Think about it tonight, and come back with some ideas for tomorrow."

Connor put up his hand. "How does an interview make society better?" he asked.

"Depends on who you interview," said Ms. Koon. "A criminal who is dumping garbage doesn't help society. But if you interview the same criminal who has reformed and is now working at a recycling plant, that shows how we can improve. Do you see? Think about something or someone that makes life better for people, makes society better."

Cody didn't care much about school projects. Usually he forgot all about them until the day they were due. Then he handed in something late and sloppy. But he found himself thinking about this one.

Who helped other people? Doctors help when you're sick. Who else? Firefighters? EMTs? He didn't know many people with those jobs. Mrs. Ahmad from down the hall always gave money to homeless guys. She'd walk down Parliament Street and give out cash to everyone who asked. That was pretty good, right?

Connor had his hand up again. "Like the crew who takes care of our garden and lawns?" he said. "They make our place look nicer, and they get rid of weeds."

"Do you understand what I mean by *society*, Connor?" asked Ms. Koon.

"Like my house isn't part of society?"

"Only a small part, Connor. You want to think bigger."

"The crew takes care of other houses in the neighborhood."

Cody could hear Autumn sigh from across the room.

"We'll talk more about this tomorrow," said Ms. Koon.

The bell rang to end the school day.

Cody and Autumn walked together. She was walking back home. He was walking back to . . . not "home," exactly, but he was starting to think that he belonged there. For now. For a little while. Whatever that meant.

It was a sunny, windy afternoon. Small clouds raced across the sky. The blue-and-white flag sticking out of the porch of the corner house rippled loudly. They talked about the social studies project. Well, Cody did. Autumn wasn't paying much attention.

"What about the community center?" he said. "You know, the place we went on Saturday and gave out lunches. Feeding people is good for society, right?"

"Uh-huh," said Autumn.

"I could do my project on that. Maybe interview some of the people there. What do you think?"

She sprinted ahead for a few seconds, then jogged back to him. "What did you say, Cody?"

"Nothing."

She looked over her shoulder. "Let's have a race."

"What? Where?"

"You and me. Now. I'll run backward and you run forward." She checked over her shoulder again. No one was coming toward them on the sidewalk. "Ready? Set? Go!"

She took off into the wind, stepping high, elbows pumping, smiling back at him. "Come on, slowpoke!"

He started after her. She sped up. He couldn't catch her, even though she was running backward. They ran for half a block or so before she stumbled, caught herself, and turned around to walk forward.

"Wow, you're good," he panted.

"Not as good as I used to be. I'm out of breath already."

She didn't seem out of breath. Cody was gasping like a fish in the bottom of a boat.

The house across the street from Autumn's had lots going on today. Two men stood on top of scaffolding, trying to maneuver a long beam into a window on the second floor of the house. A backhoe dug in the front garden. A sheet of dark green canvas hung down the front of the scaffolding. It rippled in the breeze. The writing on it was bold and easy to read: ACME RENOVATION—GOOD FOR ALL OF US.

Autumn started to laugh. "Connor could do his social studies project on them," she said.

AUTUMN

After dinner, Autumn and Cody did the dishes together. He rinsed and scraped, and she loaded the dishwasher because he didn't know where everything went yet. Cody, who had apparently gotten over his shyness, talked about his ideas for his social studies project and who he'd most like to talk to at the community center. He was actually smiling, which made him look much less ratlike than usual. His eyes weren't constantly moving as if he expected someone to jump out and hit him.

"I want to start by interviewing your mom," he told Autumn, handing her a salad bowl. "Do you think she'd talk to me about the center?"

"Uh-huh." The more Autumn thought about it, the more she liked Cody's idea. Not that she wanted to steal it from him. But between the two of them, maybe they could put together something pretty amazing.

And if she was being honest, she didn't really have a good idea of her own.

She wasn't in the same bizarro league as Connor, who thought interviewing his gardener was a groundbreaking idea. But other than the community center, Autumn didn't really do much that made any kind of difference to anyone. She thought back to all the weekends she had skipped going to the community center because she had slept at Mia's house or gone to watch Connor play soccer instead, and she was ashamed. Maybe if she and Cody brought some attention to the community center and the people who worked there . . . maybe she could make up for it somehow.

"So . . ." She cleared her throat. "I kinda thought . . . I mean, I wondered if maybe . . ." Why was this so hard? "I wondered if I could help you."

"What do you mean?" He handed her a water glass. Autumn fumbled and almost dropped it.

"I thought maybe we could do the project together. If you wanted to." Autumn couldn't look at him. Which was weird because she was used to taking control of stuff like this. But this new, outgoing version of Cody threw her off. And he was studying her intently, which was also kind of off-putting. "I mean, we don't have to. I can find something else to do. It's just that the community center was my thing first," she finished. Oh God. She sounded like Mia. "I mean . . . that's totally not what I meant! I just thought . . ." She trailed off, feeling like the biggest jerk in the world.

But Cody was smiling at her. She had literally seen him smile more today than in the entire time they'd gone to school together.

"Yeah! Actually, that would be cool. You already know everyone, so you can help figure out who we should talk to and make sure they're okay with it. I figure they'd be happier talking to you anyway, since you've been going there for so long and I just started."

"Really? Yeah! Cool! I could totally do that!"

It was weird. She looked at Cody smiling widely at her and didn't feel the quick tug of anger and resentment she usually felt when she looked at him.

"We have to plan. It's due next week, and we should know who we want to talk to when we go back to the center," Connor said.

"We can make a list after we're done here. Do you think we should just hand in a video?"

"Maybe. What do you think? I was thinking I'd do some kind of cover art," he said shyly. He had been working in the studio with her dad, so Autumn knew he liked to draw and paint. And she liked to write, so this could actually be a pretty good partnership.

"Okay. Well, what if we present it like an article? We'll both do the interviews and then I can write it up and you can do the artwork?"

"Yeah. That would work."

They finished the dishes chatting excitedly about the project, what they'd each contribute and who they should talk to the next day.

It was almost like they had become . . . maybe not friends . . . not yet. But they at least had settled into some kind of peace.

CODY

So much had happened so fast! Over the last few days, every hour had been full of new things. Bad things, like Dad beating him so hard he had to leave. Good things, like Autumn taking him in. Then more bad things, like him being mean and wrong to the Bird family. Then weird things, like Dad moving without telling him, and visiting Mom and her freaking out at Mr. Bird. Then more good things, like learning to draw. Then Autumn losing her school friends and calling him a racist. And then him and Autumn becoming, well, friends. Friendly enough to come up with a school project to do together. Imagine that, eh—what would Dad say? Honestly, it seemed like the last few days had taken a year.

By contrast, the rest of the week passed in a rush. On Tuesday, Ms. Koon agreed that Autumn and Cody could work on the project together. That evening, Cody interviewed Autumn's mom about the community center, with Autumn holding the camera steady while he read the questions the two of them had made up.

On Wednesday, her dad helped Cody plan his sketch of the

community center that was going to be part of the project.

"Take a picture of the scene you want to draw," he said. "The visual will help with perspective and proportion." They drove to the center on Wednesday. Mr. Bird parked a few doors away, in a No Parking zone.

Cody had his new phone ready. He knew what he wanted to draw. He crossed to the south side of Wellesley Street so he could get a picture of the entrance doors and front window. He waited for a lull in traffic. He pressed the button. There was a satisfying *click*.

Cody had taken his first-ever picture with his first-ever phone. He checked the shot. It was blurry. And there was a blob in the middle, blocking the door handle. Was it a bird? It looked like it might be a bird. Cody tried again. He waited until the scene was clear of cars and pedestrians and held the phone up in front of him. Pause. Press. *Click.* Another picture.

This one was pretty blurry too—either he was a terrible photographer or this phone had a lousy camera. And, wouldn't you know it, there was another bird in the picture! Or maybe the same one. Weird.

A car horn made Cody look up. Mr. Bird was beckoning urgently. A police officer was getting out of his car and looking at Mr. Bird's. Cody dashed across the street and slid into the passenger seat.

"Sorry," he said.

"Just on our way, Officer," said Mr. Bird in a loud, clear voice, putting the car in gear and driving away.

For the next two days, Cody hardly saw Autumn except at school and meals. He spent all his spare time working on the community center sketch. He used the phone picture to set out the composition. He followed Mr. Bird's instructions to keep his wrist loose and to let his mind go free. "Charcoal is a great drawing tool," he told Cody over and over. "You can't erase your mistakes, so you learn not to worry about them. Work with the tool. Use what it gives you."

After a few false starts, Cody got the front of the building okay, and the window. He tried to ignore the bird smudge, but it appeared in his picture as he drew. In fact, the more he worked around it, the clearer it got. It was a crow. Cody didn't know why it was there, but he didn't draw over it.

In social studies on Friday, last period of the week, Autumn had an announcement. She stood at the front of the room with a big brown envelope.

"Tomorrow is Saturday," she said.

"Look who's been doing her homework," snarked Mia. "Do you know the name of the day after that?"

The class laughed. Autumn ignored Mia and carried on.

"Every Saturday at noon, the community center on Wellesley has an open house, with a free meal and a chance to socialize. My family has been part of it for years. Last Saturday, Cody showed up to help out."

The class broke up when someone—maybe Mia, maybe Aliyah—made a loud kissy noise and everyone else went, "Ooooooh!"

Cody blushed. Ms. Koon, who was pretty chill, told everyone to settle down. Autumn sighed and shook her head.

"Cody and I are doing our social studies project together, and we thought we'd invite you all be part of it too. The timing is amazing. This Saturday's open house marks the tenth anniversary of the community center. My mom is on the planning board, and they've been working with the mayor's office and the police. Starting at noon on Saturday, Wellesley Street will be closed so they can have tables outside. CityTV is coming, and celebrities are going to work behind the counters and serve meals. In this envelope"—she held it up—"are passes for anyone who wants to help us out."

The class gasped all together: twenty people, twenty gasps.

Someone said, "Wow."

Someone else started clapping. Ms. Koon joined in, and soon the whole class was applauding madly.

Everyone took a ticket. Even Connor. Even Mia.

"Parliament and Wellesley? Eww," said Connor.

"Who are the celebrities?" Mia asked. "Anyone I've heard of?"

Autumn smiled and didn't answer.

Cody was as surprised as anyone by Autumn's announcement. Dr. Bird had mentioned the ten-year anniversary thing during the interview. Autumn must have been busy for the last couple of days.

"So that's what you've been doing," he said on the way back to her place. Home. "Getting the passes. Talking to the mayor. You're pretty organized. I didn't know about any of that stuff."

It was raining lightly. Cody had his new hoodie on. Autumn was in shirtsleeves. She was walking backward to strengthen whatever muscles get strengthened when you do that.

"Mom told us some of it yesterday," she said. "I told you the rest this morning. You knew about all of it, Cody. You just weren't paying attention."

"Oh."

"The idea for the project was yours. You did as much as I did."

"So, what celebrities are coming?"

"I don't know if any are. I made that bit up, to see if they'd jump at it."

Cody's mouth dropped open. He laughed and laughed.

A few houses down he said, "Wouldn't it be something if sports stars showed up. Maple Leafs and Blue Jays and Raptors?"

She smiled. "And Drake. He likes the Raptors."

"Drake!"

Cody heard a barely contained gasp off to his left. He noticed a furtive movement behind the hedge they were passing. He wondered.

What had Isabel overheard?

AUTUMN

Autumn woke up early on Saturday to the sun streaming through her window, promising a beautiful day for the open house. She threw her legs over the side of the bed and stretched, yawning widely. Having the news covering the open house was huge for the center. She knew they could use more volunteers, and funding would be a bonus. It didn't hurt that it would be great for her project too. And if she was being honest, she wanted the other kids to see how lucky they were to have the latest video games and the most expensive sneakers.

She dressed quickly, pulled her hair into a ponytail, and grabbed a hoodie from her closet, before ducking into the bathroom to splash some water on her face and brush her teeth. She could smell pancakes before she got to the kitchen, and her stomach gurgled hungrily.

Cody was already stuffing a huge serving of pancakes drowning in syrup down his gullet when she pulled a chair up to the table and took two from the pile.

"You look like you've never had pancakes before," she told

him, then blushed because it occurred to her that it was highly possible he hadn't.

But Cody just grinned through his mouthful and wiped syrup off his chin.

Maybe a visit to the center was something she needed to experience today too.

The street was already blocked off when Autumn and her family drove up, and there were news vans and crowds of people surrounding the center. Her dad stepped out to talk to a police officer, who moved the barricade out of the way so they could park behind the building.

"Do you think any celebrities are here?" Cody whispered.

"Mom said they were talking to the Raptors organization. But I don't think we'll see a star," Autumn whispered back.

She knew her classmates would be looking for someone famous to take selfies with. There was Mia, being shadowed by Aliyah and Isabel. "Let's go in the back."

"Why? Everyone's out front," Cody said.

"BECAUSE everyone's out front! Do you want to explain to Mia and Connor and everyone why the biggest celebrity serving food out there is the guy who wears the hot dog costume at the barbecue place?"

"There's a guy who wears a hot dog costume? Where?"

"Oh, for the . . . Just come with me!" Autumn pulled him in through the back door, where they were immediately swallowed into a chaotic crush of volunteers, regulars, and press.

"Autumn!" one of the senior volunteers called out, then turned to the reporter setting up beside him. "If you want to talk to someone, you should talk to Autumn. She's been volunteering here for years with her parents."

"Oh, really?" The reporter looked at Autumn with interest. "Would you be willing to talk to me about your experience here at the center?" she asked.

"Yeah, sure. Just let me . . ." She trailed off as she caught sight of Connor with his buddies, wrinkling his nose and pointing at Martha, one of the regulars, before the boys doubled over laughing. Autumn changed directions and headed over to them. "Do you want to go with Cody and get some tea, Martha?" she asked kindly, smiling at the woman she had known most of her life and taking her hand gently.

"All right," Martha agreed.

"Cody, can you find somewhere for Martha to sit and bring her a cup of tea, please?" she asked him.

"Sure." He nodded and led Martha back toward the tables set up near the kitchen.

Autumn spun around the second Martha was out of earshot and faced Connor. "Something funny?"

"How can you stand it in here?" Connor asked, smirking.

"A lot of these people are homeless, Connor. This might be the only square meal they get in a week, and they don't need jerks like you coming in here and acting like spoiled brats. Martha has a PhD. So why don't you shut up and grab an apron?"

Autumn walked away, noting with great satisfaction the look of complete shock on Connor's face. What she didn't notice was the cameraman filming her.

CODY

What a zoo! Cody was amazed at how big the event was. Autumn's mom must have had amazing connections. Police cars blocked off Wellesley Street between Parliament and Sherbourne. Picnic tables were spread out in front of the community center. The hand-lettered bedsheet sign over the door read 10th anniversary!

A woman was setting up to play guitar on a little stage. Someone was riding a unicycle and juggling bowling pins. There was a truck and a Jeep from CityTV, and at least two people with big TV cameras filming other people with microphones. And there were hundreds of people wandering around, phones held in the air, memorializing the event.

That reminded him. He asked if he could take a picture of Martha.

"Why would you want to do that?" she asked.

"You're part of my school project."

"Your project is on poor old ladies? School has changed. When I was in school, all our projects were on Canadian history—as if life here began when the Europeans started arriving." Martha's laugh showed a lot of gaps between teeth. "All the textbooks were written by white people. Now that I think about it, doing a project on poor old ladies makes more sense."

The picnic tables on the street in front of the center were full of people. No food yet, but cutlery and napkins were piled in the center of the tables. The people were different races and ethnicities and ages and sizes. They hung around between tables like this was a trendy restaurant and they were waiting for seats. Cody helped Martha to an empty place. A lady opposite recognized her and said hello.

Cody looked around for the friendly card players from last week. He couldn't see them. But there was Dr. Bird! She waved and pointed inside. Cody gave a thumbs-up.

The kitchen was jammed full of people in aprons. Cody found a face he recognized from last week.

"Hi!" he said. "I was here last Saturday with the Birds."

"I remember you. Cody, right?"

She handed him an apron. He tied it on. "Thanks," he said. Her name came to him suddenly, like an answer to a prayer. "Thanks, Lucy!"

Her smile dazzled.

A tall, handsome guy and a short guy in glasses had a crowd of people around them. Were they celebrities? On the tall guy, the apron looked like a miniskirt. Cody didn't recognize him, but thought he could be a Raptor. The guy beside him was too old and too short to be a Raptor. He was dressed worse than the other guy, way less cool. He couldn't be famous, could he? What would he be famous for?

The cooks were working hard. Stirring pots, shaking salad, chopping vegetables, slicing bread.

Lucy clapped her hands to get attention from all the other aprons. "Lunch will be ready in a few minutes," she said. "There's going to be a town crier to open the festivities. Then you can start handing out snacks."

She gestured behind her to a long counter filled with plates of bread and raw veggies.

And there was Aliyah and Mia. Their aprons were tied with perfect bows. Beside them, Connor tried to step into his apron as if it was a pair of pants. He had clearly never worn one. Cody took some pictures.

"Who's the town crier?" asked someone.

"*What's* a town crier?" asked someone else.

The waiter beside Cody was gawking at the strangers with the crowd around them. "Look who came!" she said.

"Who is he?" asked Cody.

"Don't you watch basketball?"

"Aha! I *thought* it was basketball."

"He invented a whole new defense," she said. "He's the best coach in the league. It's so cool that he's here!"

"Wait—who are you talking about?"

"Who are *you* talking about? That's Franz Horvat in the glasses."

"So . . . who's the other guy? The tall guy?"

"Him? I dunno. Some kids' author, I think."

"What?!"

"No one I've heard of. He's cute, though."

Cody's thoughts were interrupted by a vigorous ringing from outside. Sounded like an old-fashioned school bell. The echoes died, and someone started yelling. The voice was not loud. Not LOUD. It was *LOUD*!

"HEAR YE! HEAR YE! THE CITY DECLARES THE COMMUNITY CENTER CELEBRATION IS NOW OPEN!"

Through the open door, Cody saw a guy standing on the guitar player's stage. He was wearing a long jacket, ruffled shirt, and pirate hat. Everyone in the kitchen rushed to get a picture.

Cody texted Autumn:

> **Did you get the bell ringer?**

She texted back a minute later:

> **On video. Where you?**

> **Kitchen**

> **Did you see Coach Horvat? Get his picture**

Jeez, thought Cody. *Everyone knows about this guy. Maybe he is famous, after all.*

The next hour passed quickly and pleasantly. The guitarist played. The sun shone. People ate and talked and mostly smiled. Connor and Mia looked around for TV cameras. Cody handed out food to the bridge-playing ladies from last week. Connor and Mia didn't carry any food, but the tall kids' author carried a lot. He showed Cody how to carry two plates in one hand without spilling. He knew how because he was a waiter when he wasn't writing. "You make an extra tray out of your left wrist, thumb, and baby finger, like this," he said, bending way over so Cody could see.

Cody thanked him and tried to think of a book question. He couldn't. Unless this guy wrote X-Men comics, Cody hadn't read him. Finally he asked, "Where do you get your ideas?"

The author sighed.

* * *

There was a craft table near the door, with stuff for sale to help the community center. Mostly it was clothes and games, but there were also some books and movies. An old lady had been ringing up the sales and making change throughout the lunch. A sign hung over her head. Cody smiled to himself every time he noticed it.

The sign said:

ART AUCTION 3:00 P.M.

PROCEEDS TO THE

COMMUNITY CENTER

As they started to clear away the lunch dishes, Mr. Bird came out of the kitchen carrying the forest scene Cody had woken up to for a week now. He propped it up on the craft table. With a carved wooden frame around it, it looked like something in an art gallery. Lots of people stopped eating to look at it. The CityTV crew was still filming. So was Autumn. Cody saw her at the edge of the crowd, phone in front of her.

Mr. Bird went back into the center and came out with two more pieces. One was a small picture of a bird in the snow that Cody had never seen before. It was bright and cheerful. Cody could read the signature at the bottom: *T. Bird*.

The other picture was Cody's charcoal sketch of the community center doors. It was framed too. Mr. Bird propped it next to his paintings. Like it belonged with them. Which was ridiculous.

But still.

ART AUCTION 3:00 P.M.

Cody couldn't help smiling at his picture. The doors, the sidewalk, the window. The weird smudgy bird in front. There it was. That was his work.

Autumn was still recording. All this would go into the project.

ART AUCTION 3:00 P.M.

A dark limousine pulled up to the police barricades, honking.

The guitar player stopped.

Everyone looked over.

A whisper went through the crowd.

"Do you think it's—"

"Could it be—"

A server clearing next to Cody dropped her empty plates back down on the wooden tabletop and covered her open mouth with her hand.

"It's him!" she almost shrieked.

Of course it wasn't Drake. Wrong age, wrong color, wrong hair, wrong style. Excitement whooshed out of the crowd like air out of a busted balloon.

Still, he must have been a celebrity. He had his own videographer. She pushed people out of the way so she could take video of her man walking down the street. She got him talking to the Raptors' coach and the kids' author, and the woman who ran the community center. She and her camera followed him and Autumn's mom across the street to the stage, where Dr. Bird borrowed the guitarist's microphone to introduce him. Turned out he was the mayor.

Cody checked the crowd. Ms. Koon was near the stage. Margaret, the class good girl, stood right next to the teacher because that's where Margaret usually was. Connor and Mia elbowed each other out of the way so they could wave at the TV cameras. Where was Isabel? She could be anywhere.

The mayor was talking about success and community and what a great city this was. A boring speech. Cody's attention wandered.

ART AUCTION 3:00 P.M.

Autumn had told him that Mr. Bird's paintings were worth tens of thousands of dollars. He wondered what his was worth. Tens of dollars? One dollar?

The mayor finished his speech to polite applause, shook Dr. Bird's hand and the hand of the head of the center, and walked back to his limousine, waving.

Was that it? Was the thing over?

No. The guy in the pirate hat came out from behind the stage, ringing his handbell. Cody saw him up close. He was sweating, which made sense, since he was wearing a frilly turtleneck thing and a heavy coat.

"HEAR YE, HEAR YE! LET THE CELEBRATION CONTINUE."

He bowed to the applause and stomped away down Wellesley Street.

It was early afternoon. Sun was out, people were talking. Cody headed back into the kitchen with more plates. The only waiters left were the regulars. There was a pile of aprons on a chair, including one that was still tied up. That must have been Connor's.

Cody kept his apron on. He didn't want to leave while there was still work to do. He was getting better at stacking plates now, thanks to the author.

His heart was full. This project for Ms. Koon was going to be amazing. Autumn's video today, the interview with her mom, and a copy of Cody's picture as a cover. And there was the possibility of the sale of his real picture. That would be cool. A check for any amount—even $24.95. Even $1.00.

Cody had never felt this good about any project before. In fact, he'd hardly ever felt this good before, period. He didn't know where he was going to live next year, next month, even next week. Not for sure. But he sort of guessed. He had seen Dr. and Mr. Bird look at him, look at each other. Whatever his future held, he trusted them. They wouldn't let him down.

And there was his picture! He did that!

ART AUCTION 3:00 P.M.

What was going on? A disturbance at the edge of the crowd. Someone was shoving someone else. Cody could hear raised voices. A woman and a man, and then another man. The second man's voice got louder as he got closer to the community center. He wanted his free lunch. He wanted it now.

When Cody heard the voice, his whole body froze. Like a mammoth trapped in the Ice Age. That kind of freeze. He could not move.

The voice got louder. The man got closer.

Cody stood in the doorway.

The man was close enough for Cody to make out the words he was shouting.

"What's the matter—you got rocks in your head?" He pushed someone out of the way, staggered forward, and caught himself.

He was ragged, drunk, unshaven. His eyes were so bleary he probably couldn't see well enough to tie his shoelaces, which were undone. His hair was red and dirty and hung over his forehead. His hands hung loose at his sides.

He was Cody's dad.

AUTUMN

In her whole entire life, Autumn never thought she'd see Connor wearing an apron. But there he was. Mostly doing nothing except making sure he was within shot of the cameras from the news stations that had shown up. Probably hoping this would be some kind of big break or that Drake really would show up and see him "helping out" and congratulate him and offer him courtside seats or something. She watched, stifling a laugh, as Lucy shoved a bag of trash into his hands and steered him toward the bins at the back doors.

She took some video of Coach Horvat and the children's author—she couldn't remember his name—and then ducked outside, where crowds of people waited at the tables set up for food, listened to a guitar player strumming on the stage, or stood around in groups laughing and chatting together in front of the center they had come to love.

It was pretty amazing.

She texted Cody:

> This is amazing.

He texted back:

> **I know**

Quick and to the point as always. Autumn grinned.

"Is he here?" a voice asked behind her. Mia. Autumn knew there was no way she could resist the promise of celebrities. "Isabel said Drake was coming. Where is he?"

"I don't know. Inside, maybe." Autumn turned around. Good Lord. Mia and Aliyah were slathered in enough makeup for the entire drama department at school to do their spring musical. "You know what? I bet if you went in and asked to help out, you could get into where the celebrities are hanging out."

"Really?"

"Yeah. They have them in the back where they're getting everything ready. I bet if you told them you wanted to help serve the food to everyone, you'd get to meet them all."

"Will they let us?" Mia asked, clutching Aliyah's hand excitedly. Her face barely moved, weighed down as it was with makeup.

"Sure. They can always use help serving. Just tell them I sent you."

"OHMYGOSHTHANKYOU!" Mia and Aliyah hugged

her and ran off to the center doors. There was no way she could let Cody miss this.

> **Just convinced Mia and Aliyah that if they helped serve food they could get back to where the celebrities are. If they ask go along with it**

It took a couple of minutes, but his response was worth the wait.

> **OMG!**

And a photo of Mia and Aliyah in matching aprons.

Autumn was pretty busy after that. But she did make sure to get a quick video of Mia and Aliyah serving Martha, because there was no way she ever wanted to forget that.

"Excuse me." Autumn felt a tap on her shoulder and turned around to find a woman with a microphone and a man with a huge camera on his shoulder.

"Yeah?"

"You volunteer here, don't you?"

"Yes. Do you need something?"

"Do you mind if I ask you a few questions?"

"Umm . . . wouldn't you rather talk to my mom? Or my dad? They volunteer here as well."

"I actually already talked to your mom inside. We saw you talking to another boy and telling him about how important the center is to the people it serves. I'd love to get you talking about that."

"Oh. Well, if my mom said it was okay . . . What do you want me to say?"

"Just tell us about the center."

The woman nodded at the cameraman and, within a fraction of a second, turned into a completely different person, looking into the camera and positioning herself beside Autumn.

"I'm here with Autumn Bird, a volunteer at the community center. Autumn, can you tell us what the center means to you?"

Autumn blinked at her and then the camera. Crap.

"Ummm . . . well . . ." She cleared her throat and took a deep breath. "My parents and I have been volunteering here for years. It's a place where anyone who needs a meal or a friendly face can come and hang out. We do clothing drives so that anyone in need can get clothes. And there's a pretty competitive card game that has been going on for as long as I can remember. The center is a home for a lot of people who don't have anywhere else to go. And it's a family. An amazing family." She smiled widely. Because it was. And she was proud to be part of it.

"Great. Thanks. That was perfect," the reporter told her. "I think they're wrapping things up now. Congratulations. It was a great event."

"Thanks!"

Autumn filmed the town crier, who was the loudest person she had ever heard, and got ready to go find her parents and Cody. She walked past the other volunteers cleaning up and was about to go back into the center when she was knocked into the doors by a big man who smelled like he had been drinking for a week.

"Hey!"

CODY

Dad stood in front of the center doors, swaying. His eyes weren't focusing.

"Where's my free lunch? This place"—he swung his arms around, almost losing his balance—"gives out free lunches. I want one!"

He was loud enough to be heard a long way.

Cody peered into the kitchen. Lunch was supposed to be over. Was there an extra sandwich? Just one? He saw someone nod their head. There was a flurry of activity at the long table and then the waiter who knew her basketball jogged out.

"Here you go, sir!" she said brightly, holding out the plate. "It's our last one. Chicken salad. And a date square."

Cody kept his eyes on Dad, who stared down at the plate like he didn't know what it was.

"There's a free table over there. Want to sit down?"

Dad's head whipped around as Cody spoke. His eyes widened. His breath exploded out of him in a loud grunt. He hadn't recognized his son before. Now he did. The look on his face was one Cody had seen, oh, a thousand times before.

Rage.

And no prize for guessing who he was mad at.

"You!" he said, voice grinding like a cement mixer. "What are you doing here?"

Cody was scared. Dad's rage was always scary. He tried to distract him.

"Your lunch—" he started.

Dad dropped the plate. It crashed to the pavement and broke into pieces, scattering food.

The small crowd gasped. Dad pointed at Cody with a dirty forefinger.

"You ran away! Last week. You're a rat! You're a disgrace!"

He didn't speak clearly. The last word came out *dissshgraysh*. He was not as loud as the town crier, but he was way more frightening.

The crowd drew back.

Dad's other hand—not the pointing one—was at his side, clenched into a fist. Cody cringed.

"You're mine. You don't run away. You belong to me. Right?"

Cody watched the fist.

"Right?"

The sandwich and broken plate were still on the ground.

Cody's lips froze. His tongue stuck to the roof of his mouth. He wanted to speak out, but his will had gone the same way as his voice. He couldn't—just couldn't—say no to his dad. Couldn't tell him to go away.

Someone else could.

"No," said a familiar voice.

The crowd parted to let an angry Autumn through. This was not a self-doubter, worried about her friends. This was what courage looked like. She stood with her hands on her hips and her jaw stuck out. She was not afraid of Dad. She talked quieter than he did but much clearer.

"He doesn't belong to you," she said.

Dad turned to face her, staggering slightly. "What do you know, little girl? He's my kid. He does what I say!"

Now he stepped backward and grabbed Cody clumsily and awkwardly by the hair. There were gasps from the crowd.

They talk about time standing still. It doesn't. But the world did seem to spin a little slower for Cody just then. He was in shock, encountering his dad and having the old man be as mean as before. With everything moving slower, words stretched out and became meaningless. Cody could not understand what anyone was saying.

On the other hand, he had time to notice details. Details like:

- Autumn's dark eyes, which widened and flashed with anger.

- The sun going behind a cloud, so that the day suddenly darkened.

- Dr. and Mr. Bird, who showed up together and stood beside their daughter, waving and pointing.

- Dad waving back with his free hand.

- Dad gripping Cody's hair with his other hand.

- Mr. Bird's pictures, and Cody's sketch, on the craft table under the sign: ART AUCTION 3:00 P.M.

- The constellation of cell phones flashing their lights along the length of the crowd.

- Cody's heart going *nee-naw nee-naw* like a siren on *Peppa Pig*.

How long did this episode last? How much time passed in slow motion? A fair amount. Cody noticed the *nee-naw nee-naw* sound getting louder. And louder. Turned out not to be his heart. It was an ambulance, boxy, blue and white, lights flashing.

People stopped yelling. Dad let go of his hair. The crowd and its constellation of cell phones wheeled around to track the emergency vehicle as it sped down Parliament Street. The siren faded.

Okay. Time started moving at normal speed again. Cody could understand what Dad and the Birds were saying.

"You kidnapped him," said Dad. "You're crooks!"

"No, Mr. Stouffer," said Dr. Bird. "Our daughter found him on the street and brought him home."

"Like a stray cat? Is that it? That what you think he is? A cat?"

"He's a runaway!" That was Autumn, still angry. "You hurt him! He had two black eyes. They're just getting better now!"

"So what?"

"You admit you hurt him?"

"Admit? I don't admit nothing. If I hurt him, he deserved it."

They stood in a circle on the sidewalk near the door of the community center. The crowd was mostly dispersed.

Cody was outside the circle. He watched the sky getting darker. He listened to them talking about him. He had nothing to add. He knew what was going to happen now. He'd known all along. It was always going to come to this.

"Right, boy?" His dad grabbed his shoulder, shook him. "Right, Cody? You're with me. We're going back to the Markeen Hotel. I've got the third-floor room. You don't want anything to do with these kind of people."

"*What* kind of people?" asked Autumn. "People who get drunk and hit their kids? People like you?" She laughed. Not funny *ha ha ha*, but still a laugh.

Cody could have told her what happened to Dad when you laughed at him. Sure enough, he swelled up like a ripe boil. He was going to explode. He held his arms straight down and squared off against Autumn and her family.

"You should talk about drunks!" he shouted. "I know your type, Pocahontas. Think you can laugh at me? You?"

"Hey!" said Autumn, angry.

"Hey," said Mr. Bird, quiet.

Dad was so upset there was spit coming out of his mouth. He wiped it with a trembling hand. "What? You're Indians, right? You look it. This isn't racist; I'm just saying what I see. I'm white, you're not. So you got rich off government handouts. Now you think you're better than me? Think you can laugh at me? Think you can take my kid away from me?"

"Government handouts? What are you—"

"Please, Tom," said Dr. Bird. "Let me."

When she put her hand on her husband's arm, he subsided. Cody saw them as a couple for the first time. They were together, not just individuals.

"Please listen, Mr. Stouffer," she said, calm as pudding. "I have concerns for Cody's health. His injuries last week were consistent with a physical assault. He told me you kicked him. As a medical doctor, I have responsibility. I will not put him in danger. Before you take him away—"

"Mom!"

"No, Autumn, this is an important point. Before you take Cody away, let's establish that you won't mistreat him again. And—most important of all—let's find out what he wants to do."

"Oh," said Autumn.

Dr. Bird turned toward Cody. Her smile was not sharp, like Autumn's. It was wise and distant. She was looking at him from far away and long ago. Her voice was calm.

"Take the last point first," she said. "What do you think, Cody? Do you want to go with your dad?"

It all came down to this. Cody had known his dad his whole life. He had known the Birds for a week. Dad was wrong about Autumn and her parents. He was wrong about almost everything. He could be cruel and careless.

But he was what Cody knew. And he was what Cody *understood*.

Cody had to fake it at Autumn's place. He had never seen half the things she took for granted. Not just the Indigenous stuff, but things like a bathroom of his own, or a closet full of clothes, or a TV set bigger than his old kitchen table.

Cody could add and read and navigate his own neighborhood. He could disappear into his mind so he survived in the middle of crap. But there was so much he didn't know. What was *Doctor Who*? Why couldn't you slurp soup out of the bowl? How often were you supposed to do laundry? A hundred other things. Also, the Birds were good to him, which meant he had to be grateful—and that was no fun.

Thing was, he *didn't* belong in a mansion or a clean, comfortable car. He belonged in a community center soup kitchen. He would belong with his dad in the Markeen Hotel. He knew the Markeen—a roachy, by-the-week place down on George Street.

That was what Cody was used to. That was his past. Hard to say goodbye to that. Also, Dad was not always a monster. He had taught Cody how to throw a football. The two of them used to laugh at *The Simpsons*. Saying yes to Dad might make him happy.

Cody looked around. The afternoon was seriously dark. Looked like it might rain soon. The celebration was over. The picnic tables were piled on the sidewalk. The barricades were gone. One lane of Wellesley Street was open.

His attention caught one more time on the craft table. ART AUCTION. Someone was carrying Mr. Bird's big picture inside. His smaller one was still there, and so was Cody's sketch.

He'd made that. That was cool. Learning about drawing was maybe the best part of staying with the Birds. That was something he wouldn't forget.

He wanted to walk away from his dad. He wanted to stay with the Birds. But he was afraid to say so. He was afraid he didn't deserve it.

Help. He said it inside. He didn't know who he was talking to.

Help me!

Dr. Bird stared at him. Did she see inside? Did she hear him? Did she know?

Time does not slow down when you're thinking. It speeds up. All these pictures and ideas flashed through Cody's head in a second.

He swallowed, let out his breath.

"Hey, buddy," said Autumn. "You can stay, you know. We like you."

"Thanks." It was his first speech in a while and his voice broke. He said it again. "Thanks." Getting to know her was one of the best things that had happened this week.

"Oh! And . . ." He remembered what he owed her. What he meant to say to her. This was maybe not the best time, but the idea came into his head and he spoke without thinking. "Sorry," he said. "I'm really sorry for how I thought about you before."

And Dad lost it. He exploded all over everybody. "That's enough!" he shouted. "That. Is. Enough. Who do you think you are? No *witch doctor* is going to tell me I can't take my kid. You have concerns? Stick your concerns in your papoose! As for you, boy, I don't care what you think. You're mine. Let's go!"

He grabbed Cody by the upper arm and pulled him onto the road.

"No!" shouted Autumn. "No! Stop! You horrible man!"

Cody's dad turned back. She was looking left and right, getting ready to run after him.

And then—

And then, from behind Autumn and off to the side, a dark shape flashed past and out into the road. A leaf? No, it was too big and moving too fast. A bird? Weird. Where did it come from?

Wellesley Street was mostly empty. Dad pulled Cody across, stopping to let a couple of cars go by. Another one was coming. They waited.

In that instant, Cody heard a swishing, whooshing, sighing, flapping sound right in his ear. He ducked. Next instant, Dad stumbled and let go of him.

"Ow!"

Cody stared.

The whooshing was from the bird. And the bird was attacking his dad, flapping in his face, opening its beak to make croaking, cawing sounds.

"Ow!" Dad said again, waving his hands. "Get away, you—"

He grabbed Cody. The bird swooped around Dad, cawing, pecking at his hair. Did it think the hair was food?

Cody was startled but not afraid at all. It was as though he felt that the bird was *somehow—some* incomprehensible *how—* on his side.

All this was happening in the middle of Wellesley Street. No traffic in the westbound lanes.

Dad let go of Cody again to try to beat the bird away. Cody stood still, watching, waiting.

The bird was a crow. It kept cawing, attacking fiercely, forcing Dad to take a step away from it. Into the eastbound lane.

The car that hit him was not going very fast. When the driver realized that the crazy hand-waving pedestrian had moved into her lane, she slammed on the brakes, slowing some more. But even a few kilometers an hour is fast enough to do harm when you weigh as much as a car. Dad ended up splayed out on the pavement like a rag doll as it started to rain.

Police and ambulance arrived in minutes. The EMTs put Cody's dad on a stretcher and headed for the hospital, siren wailing. *Nee-naw nee-naw.*

Cody's mind drifted into a *Peppa Pig* memory, where the police car was checkered yellow and black, like the Children's Aid vans Dad had threatened Cody with if he ever complained about him.

Dad was such a liar! Cody's fear faded like the siren as the ambulance drove farther away. *Nee-naw nee-naw* nothing.

Cody and the driver of the car gave their statements inside the community center.

The driver was in shock because she'd hurt someone, even though witnesses and the police officer assured her that it was not her fault.

Cody was in shock too. Partly because, well, Dad was right beside him when he got hit. Scary stuff.

Overall, he was happy to put Dad out of his mind for now. Dad would be fine. Meanwhile, Cody wouldn't be living at the Markeen Hotel. He'd stay with the Birds instead.

He was okay with that. More than okay.

The real shock for Cody was not about the accident to his father. It was his sketch.

Autumn noticed the difference when they carried the pictures into the center, out of the rain.

"I don't remember any red," she said.

It was two hours later.

The police officer and the car driver were gone. Cody's sketch and Mr. Bird's two paintings were displayed on a table by the back wall of the community center, ready for the auction this afternoon.

Cody and Autumn waited by the table while her parents talked to the online auctioneer. Cody peered at his sketch again. He couldn't get over the change.

"You *sure* you didn't do it?" Autumn had asked this already.

"It's charcoal. Black and white. No red."

"Well, there's red now."

Cody's sketch was based on that photo he took. The small blur in the middle of the photo turned into a bird as he drew. He left it in because you can't erase charcoal, and anyway, it looked interesting.

The bird was still there. But now it held a wisp of something red in its beak.

Clearly red. Unmistakably red.

Maybe string.

Maybe red hair.

AUTUMN

As if this mystery about Cody's drawing wasn't enough to keep her up at night for the next year or so, Autumn couldn't shake the horrible sight of his dad getting hit by that car. The way it spun him around, away from Cody, and left him sprawled in the middle of Wellesley Street.

And where had that bird come from?

She knew his father wasn't a nice man. All she had to do was look at Cody's face to see that. But seeing him there, pulling Cody by the hair . . . she couldn't just sit and watch him drag Cody away to die in some dungeon somewhere. Because Autumn was pretty sure that's what would happen if Cody had left with him. Maybe not today or tomorrow. But Cody wouldn't survive.

So she'd stepped up.

Her heart had been pounding in her throat, and she could feel her hands shaking. But she pushed her way through the crowd of people who were doing nothing except watching that big hulk drag his son away by the hair, and she stood up to him.

Stood in front of him so close she could smell the liquor on his breath and see the veins in his bloodshot eyes, and she told him to stop.

For a kid she wouldn't have given her seat on the bus to a couple of weeks ago.

Then that weird crow had come out of nowhere—literally nowhere—and attacked.

Autumn Bird and the crow.

They made quite a team.

"Maybe we should have the auction another day," Autumn's mother said to the people who were still gathered around outside when the ambulance sped away with Cody's father strapped to a gurney inside.

He was going to be fine. And he'd probably be back. But that was something they could deal with later.

"No way!" Autumn called out from the back of the room, where she was perched on a chair beside Cody. "Dad and Cody worked hard on their art and they deserve to be seen. We can't let some drunk guy—sorry, Cody—stop us from having the art auction."

"Someone got hit by a car, Autumn," her mother reminded her. As if she needed reminding.

"Yes, I know. But he's fine. Or he will be. And the reporters are all still here. We had really good interest in the online auction. People can join from anywhere and we might lose some of them if we have to reschedule."

Cody looked up from his seat in the corner, where he was trying to stay out of everyone's way. As if it had been his fault or something.

"I don't know," Autumn's mom said.

"I think it's pretty smart, actually," her dad said, standing up beside his wife. "The center needs as much attention as we can get it. It's already going to be in the news because of the accident. Let's take control of the narrative and turn it into a positive."

"Will that work?" someone asked. "Or will it just bring us more bad press?"

"All press is good press!" Autumn called out. Well, that's what people said, anyway. "And even if that isn't true, we can use the attention to our advantage. Someone can go talk to the reporters and let them know."

"You should do it," Cody said, clearing his throat. "I think it should be Autumn."

"Yeah, Autumn!" came a voice from the left side of the room, followed by more people cheering. She looked at her parents, who nodded their agreement.

"Then let's get this auction started."

The room erupted with cheers as Autumn snapped some

photos and posted them on the center's account. She tagged as many people as she could think of and, followed by her family, went outside to talk to the reporters.

"So we're going to carry on with the auction as planned today. Everyone share widely. You can bid on some amazing art by my dad, Tom Bird, and by up-and-coming artist Cody Stouffer. All proceeds will go to benefit the center and the people who rely on it every single day. Thank you."

Autumn smiled and waited for the reporters to turn away before she turned and looked at her family. Her parents were nodding proudly, and Cody nudged her with his shoulder.

"Up-and-coming artist?" He grinned.

CODY

Cody couldn't remember ever being this excited. The family was back inside the community center. Dr. and Mr. Bird. Autumn. Him. Yes, he was part of the family. For now.

The center was set up for the art auction. The tables had been cleared away. In the open space were easels for Mr. Bird's paintings and Cody's drawing, and a small table with a computer for online bids. Facing them was a video camera, because the whole thing was going to be streamed.

Dr. and Mr. Bird sat in chairs off to the side of the room, sipping tea and talking with the center staff. Autumn stood near the auctioneer, who was typing fast and talking into her headset. Cody paced into the kitchen and back out, then back to the kitchen.

The clock in the kitchen said 2:45.

The auction started in fifteen minutes.

"Hey, Cody!" called Autumn. "Get this!"

She had the local news channel on her phone. They were showing a clip from this afternoon.

"That's you!"

The Raptors' coach smiled into the camera, but Cody was in the background, carrying a plate. *Weird,* he thought.

The next shot was even weirder. There was Autumn herself, staring right out at him. And there was her name on screen. Autumn Bird.

Wow.

She smiled quietly. He couldn't tell if she was pleased or embarrassed. The news switched to the prime minister giving a speech.

Cody paced to the kitchen again.

Three o'clock.

His heart skipped a beat, then started again, louder than usual. He paced back.

The auctioneer told everyone to be quiet, turned on a standing lamp beside the camera, started the camera, went back to the table, and declared the charity auction open. She had a loud, chirpy voice—like a small animal shouting at the top of its lungs. An angry mouse.

The first piece for sale was Mr. Bird's small one.

"Let's start the bidding at two thousand," suggested the auctioneer, typing busily. The light flashed off her heavy glasses.

Cody choked. Art was expensive. He remembered his dad getting upset when the price of potato chips went up.

"Thank you, artlover," said the auctioneer. "How about

three thousand? Thank you, jacobsroom. Can anyone make it four thousand? Yes, I'll take four thousand from gallerygastrohouse. How about an advance on four thousand? Thomas Bird is one of the most respected artists in Canada. His work is in galleries around the world. That's ten thousand from torontoraps. Thanks. Can we try fifteen thousand? Thank you again. That's more like it. Okay, how about—"

It was like listening to one end of a phone conversation. The auctioneer talked and typed at the same time, keeping a running total.

Autumn logged into the auction and reported back to Cody. "There are nine hundred and fifty-one people online now," she whispered.

The bidding on the first piece took another few minutes. There weren't nine hundred and fifty-one bidders—more like twenty. A few names came up again and again. Cody wondered who they all were. Was @torontoraps the coach he met that afternoon or someone else from the team or a random basketball fan?

The painting sold to @artlover for a whole lot more than the opening bid. After the auctioneer squeaked, "Sold!" Mr. Bird came over to the table to wave a thank-you to @artlover.

The next item for auction was Cody's sketch. His heart

skipped another beat when the auctioneer beckoned him over so the audience could see him.

He stood beside her and waved awkwardly. Mr. Bird went behind him, took Cody's sketch off the easel, and held it up to the camera.

In the picture, the crow still looked perky. Still had that red hair in its beak.

Cody wondered where he'd be now if he hadn't sketched it. Where he'd be if not for that crow.

"Cody Stouffer is a protégé of Tom Bird's," said the auctioneer into her headset, "so any bid you make will be an investment in the future of Canadian art as well as a real help to the community center."

Cody looked at Mr. Bird and mouthed, "Protégé?"

He nodded and smiled. Cody wondered what a protégé was.

The auctioneer turned to him. Her glasses made her look like a cheerful bug. "Before we start, we should tell our bidders the name of the picture. What do you call your sketch, Cody?"

He had not thought of a title. He had not even thought about the picture needing a title. His mind was blank.

And then, into that blank mind, like a feather into an empty sky, floated an idea.

"*Crow the Savior*," he said.

He heard a gasp coming from the side of the room, where Autumn stood with her mom.

"*Crow the Savior.*" The auctioneer typed. "Can you explain?"

Cody shrugged. "Crow saved me. That's all."

Cody made his way back to Autumn.

The auctioneer threw open the bidding at fifty dollars. Way more than he would have asked.

No one bid.

Cody sighed. Of course not.

He was standing beside Autumn. He noticed her hands because she was holding them in front of her. Her fingers were crossed.

"No bids?" said the auctioneer. "No bids for *Crow the Savior*? No bids at fifty dollars for *Crow the Savior* by—"

She stopped.

"Thank you, @kooneducator. Fifty is the price. Does anyone have an advance on fifty dollars? Can we bring it up to sixty? Remember, the money will help support the community center on Wellesley Street in Toronto, which has been operating for ten years."

"That's Ms. Koon, right?" whispered Cody to Autumn.

"Uh-huh."

"She's going to pay fifty dollars for something I drew? She must feel sorry for me."

"Maybe. Or maybe she likes it. Anyway, it means we're going to get a good mark on the project."

The auctioneer checked her timer.

"Okay," she said. "Fifty dollars going once . . . going twice . . ."

Cody let out a breath he'd been holding.

"And we have a new bid. Fifty-five dollars from a new bidder. Thank you, jumpman. Welcome to the charity auction. Tom Bird's masterpiece, *Forest Scene*, will be on the block shortly. Meanwhile, the price of Cody Stouffer's *Crow the Savior* is now fifty-five. Fifty-five dollars—make that sixty. Thank you, kooneducator."

"Jumpman?" whispered Autumn. "Do you know that word? I do. Where do I know it from?"

Cody shook his head.

"Sorry," said the auctioneer. "I think you mistyped, jumpman. Could you reenter your bid?"

Autumn squeezed Cody's upper arm. Gosh, she was strong. She thrust her phone in his face. It showed the auction website.

"What's the problem—ohhh."

He saw the new bid, reentered, from jumpman.

The auctioneer was typing furiously. "You registered with auction credit, of course . . . Just let me check . . . yes. That's fantastic. Thanks for your bid, jumpman. The new price for *Crow the Savior* is now ten thousand dollars."

Cody's heart was beating like a drum solo.

Mr. Bird laughed out loud. "Crow can be a joker," he said.

Two community center workers stood in the kitchen door, talking excitedly about music. "That's it!" Autumn whispered. "That's where I know it. 'Jumpman' is a Drake song."

"So?" said Cody.

"I know the song. There's a crow call running through it. *Caw caw.* That must be why this guy is so interested."

The workers were talking about who @jumpman could be.

"Do you think?" Autumn whispered, turning around.

"It's the kind of thing he does," said one of them. "Remember the scene in the 'God's Plan' video?"

Cody was still processing the information. Someone was going to pay ten thousand for something he did. He remembered Dad's words. *You are nothing.* Dad was in the hospital now. But if he was here, Cody would have told him how wrong he was.

He stared at the picture again. That crow looked pretty pleased.

The auctioneer said, "Going once . . . going twice . . . sold to jumpman for ten thousand dollars. The Wellesley Community Center thanks you sincerely. You can come down and pick up the work any time, or we will deliver it to your address."

Poor Ms. Koon.

The room broke into applause. Autumn turned, phone in hand, and gave Cody a hug. He hugged her back. His eyes were full.

The main event of the evening was the auction of Mr. Bird's *Forest Scene*. The auctioneer started the bidding at fifty thousand dollars.

Cody was still fighting the urge to cry. He paced back and forth as the price for Mr. Bird's painting rose.

There was a commotion from the front of the room. People gathered at the window, whispering, pointing out at Wellesley Street. The two kitchen guys hurried over to check. The auction proceeded in the background.

"Thank you, teitelgallery. What do you say, mundingerart? Tom Bird is an artist whose work has sold for six figures. As an investment alone, this would be a—thank you. We're at the assessed value of the work now. Can I find another twenty thousand dollars? There are galleries from across Canada here. What about you, WAG?"

Cody peered through the window. The car parked outside was big and bulbous, with a long hood and rounded back end. It looked like something the King of England would drive around in. Details were easy to make out because that car was parked right under a streetlight. Its hood ornament was a silver woman, bent like she was about to dive into a swimming pool.

The kitchen guys were pointing. "He drives one of those. I saw him getting out of it on TV. He's got a parking spot next to the players, near Jurassic Park."

"It's him!" said the other guy. "It was him bidding. I knew it! I knew it! He's come to get his picture."

They grabbed Cody—two guys he didn't even know—and told him how cool this all was. They gave him a thumbs-up.

"Sold!" said the auctioneer in the background.

Cody and his two new friends stared out the window. The car door opened.

AUTUMN

TWO MONTHS LATER...

"Come on! The movie is about to start! What are you guys even doing in there?" Autumn yelled out as she took the best spot on the couch and patted the spot beside her so Boomer would jump up.

"I was looking for that big bar of chocolate your mother thinks I don't know about," her dad answered, balancing an enormous bowl of popcorn and an equally large bowl of ketchup-flavored chips.

"Did you find it?" Autumn grinned.

"You know I didn't," he mourned, handing her the bowl of chips.

"Where does she hide her stash? I swear she has a secret pantry or something." Autumn laughed.

"I'll never tell," her mom said from the kitchen, tossing a chocolate bar at her and another at her dad.

Friday night at the Bird house was movie night. Snacks. Comedies usually. And no phones or guests allowed. Strictly family time.

"Where's Cody?" Autumn asked. "He's going to miss the opening credits!"

"I'm coming," Cody called out from the hallway. "I just have to wash the paint off my hands."

"I'm not saving you any chips," Autumn said, stuffing a handful in her mouth.

"I'm here. What did I miss?" He shoved himself into a spot beside Boomer, who immediately rested his head on Cody's leg and thumped his tail.

"Nothing." Autumn passed the bowl of chips over to him. "You didn't miss anything."

Family night. Autumn smiled. Who would have thought?

ACKNOWLEDGMENTS

No book is a solitary endeavor, and this one less than most. Knowing that my partner had my back (i.e., she'd have to deal with it) was a real comfort as I wrote on into an unknown plot future. And speaking of backs, the team at Scholastic has been a huge support—sales, marketing, schools, production, distribution, Diane, Anne, Erin, Yvonne, right to the front desk, everyone. On a personal note, shout out to my agent, Hilary McMahon, at WCA for pushing hard, to early reader Gayle Friesen for asking, "Are you sure?" a couple of times, and to my son Sam, whose SEO knowledge led us to the title. I love having kids who know more than me!

—Richard

I hate doing acknowledgments, but this book absolutely deserves them. I echo Richard in thanking our awesome team (he's already named all of you) at Scholastic. What a ride it has been. Anne, thanks so much for trusting us. You're amazing. Another huge thanks to Richard for being a true partner in this. I've loved everything about it (except writing without an outline—what the heck, dude?). To Amy Tompkins, my incredible agent at Transatlantic, your support has meant the world to me. And speaking of support, my milk and cookies buddies Paul Coccia, Natasha Deen, and Heather Smith, what would I do without you? No, really. What? Because your friendship and support and encouragement has gotten me through so much. So grateful for you. Almost forgot to thank my family! Chris, Josh, and Taylor, you make my life exponentially better.

—Melanie

MELANIE FLORENCE is an award-winning writer of Cree and Scottish heritage based in Toronto. Her close relationship with her grandfather sparked her interest in writing about Indigenous themes and characters. She's best known for her picture books, *Missing Nimâmâ* and *Stolen Words*, which won the 2016 TD Canadian Children's Literature Award and the 2018 Ruth and Sylvia Schwartz Children's Book Award, respectively.

Photo © 2015 Mark Raynes Roberts

RICHARD SCRIMGER is the award-winning author of more than twenty books, including *Zomboy, Lucky Jonah,* and *Downside Up*. He is also a contributor to the popular Seven series. When he's not writing or talking about writing, Richard teaches at Humber College and gets laughed at by his children. He lives in Toronto.